W9-AEM-057

GIRLS IN THE Grass

GIRLS

IN THE Grass

STORIES BY
Melanie Rae Thon

RANDOM HOUSE

NEW YORK

Some of the stories in this work were originally published elsewhere:
"Sisters" in *Antaeus*, "Girls in the Grass" in *Cutbank*,
"Repentance" in *Great River Review*, "Iona Moon" in *Hudson Review*,
"Chances of Survival" in *Iowa Review*, "Punishment" in *Southern Review*, and
"Snake River" in *Ontario Review*.

Library of Congress Cataloging-in-Publication Data
Thon, Melanie Rae.
Girls in the grass : stories / by Melanie Rae Thon.
p. cm.
ISBN 0-394-57663-2
I. Title.
PS3570.H6474G57   1991
813'.54—dc20   90-53478

Manufactured in the United States of America
2 4 6 8 9 7 5 3
First U.S. Edition

Designed by Oksana Kushnir

For my brother and sisters:
Gary, Wendy, and Laurie;
and for Bruce

ACKNOWLEDGMENTS

I am grateful to the editors who originally published individual stories included in this collection: Daniel Halpern, Paula Deitz, David Hamilton, Lynn Nankivil, Orval A. Lund, Jr., Craig Holden, Raymond J. Smith, and James Olney. I am also grateful to DeWitt Henry, Don Lee, and Wendy Lesser for their support.

I wish to thank my agent, Irene Skolnick, and my editor, Susan Kamil, for their encouragement and guidance.

Contents

GIRLS
IN THE
Grass

Girls in the Grass

*W*E'RE SITTING IN the bleachers at the Little League ballpark. No one's playing ball, but some kids with a stick pretend. We have a game for after dusk, Truth or Dare.

Truth, Meg says.

So we ask her, did you ever let a boy feel you, there? Lyla and I each put a hand on one of Meg's thighs and inch our way toward the place we mean. The question is on our minds a lot, since we start ninth grade in three months.

Yes, Meg says. She giggles, bats our hands away.

Who? says Lyla. How many times?

Meg reminds her of the rules: one question at a time.

Lyla and I wait, hungry as pups, for Meg's turn to

come around again, but the next time, Meg takes a dare instead. We think and think. It has to be good. We tell her to climb up the bleachers from underneath, hang from her knees off one of the struts, and shoot us the moon. She doesn't argue. None of us ever does. That's why we play.

Meg empties her pockets into my hands: three rusty nuts, two dimes, and a slug. As she scrambles up the underside we hear her monkey cries. She's skinny and quick. Nothing scares her. She puts her legs over the strut, swings down backward and loosens her belt. In the shadows, her thick hair falls, as coarse and tangled and dark as deer moss in the woods.

For half a minute she struggles with her jeans, wriggling out of them to show us what we want to see. Finally she dangles there, with her pants pushed up almost to her knees. The ballpark lights glint through the slats of the bleachers and the smooth globes of her bottom are striped, white and black.

Behind the old pine trees in Meg's yard, Lyla and Meg and I practice. I always have to be the boy because I'm the tall, lanky one.

Girls should make their kisses dry, Lyla tells us. Boys don't like slobber. Part your lips, she says to Meg. There, like that, and don't let them feel your tongue.

Boys can do whatever they want, that's what I think. I've kissed two boys. One's tongue twisted all over inside

4

my mouth, like it had a mind of its own and wanted to wrestle. The other boy opened his mouth so wide he got my nose and lips inside of it and I couldn't wait to catch my breath and wipe my face. I don't kiss like that when I'm being the boy, but I always try to slip my tongue between Lyla's and Meg's tense lips. It's nice when it's a little wet. And it's nice when they forget themselves and let my tongue dart in just far enough to feel where the skin of their mouths becomes as soft as the flesh of a grape.

Sometimes I get carried away and they say, not so far, close your lips, don't use your tongue like that, it tickles. They babble on and on and I let them because I know that when they've had their say, they'll both take turns kissing me again.

Meg can't stand still when she kisses. Her bony knees jab into mine, her sharp shoulders poke my breasts. She has no breasts at all, but I see her nipples perk up when we're practicing. They're so hard that even through our shirts I feel them brush against my chest.

Lyla takes kissing seriously. She says she's a professional. When I put my arms around her, she goes limp, like some daffy redhead in the movies, and I have to help her stand. Boys like that, she explains. I shrug. Maybe they do. She sighs. Before our lips even touch, Lyla lets out a sweet, low moan.

Summer's almost over when Meg tells us her family is moving to California before school starts. To Lyla and me, California might as well be New York. It's all the same. They're both farther than we'll ever go. We try to imagine sand as white as Montana snow. We picture Meg holding hands with a boy whose hair is golden and whose skin is bronze. We've seen photographs of California boys and they all look like that. The only brown-skinned boys we ever see have stringy black hair. They drive up from the reservation on Friday nights to crack nuts and drink beer at the saloon.

I'll visit, says Meg. I'll come next summer. You'll see.

But Lyla and I know that no one who leaves this place halfway between nowhere and the Canadian border ever has a good enough reason to come back.

My parents play bridge Thursday nights. Thursday is Meg's last day, so Lyla and I plan a party. I plead with Mom. We won't make a mess. We'll go to bed early. We won't cause Noreen any trouble. Noreen is my sister. She's three years older. She smokes cigarettes and wears pantyhose. Whenever she leaves the house, she stops in the alley and takes out her compact mirror to put on lipstick and mascara where our daddy won't see.

Lyla says we should invite the twins, otherwise it won't seem like a real party. Besides, we've all known the twins since we were about two. The twins don't look enough alike to even be sisters. One's pretty, with hair the color of wheat in the late afternoon. Her skin is rosy and her lips are bright. The other one is a pale towhead with eyebrows so light they disappear, but you never see the two of them apart and everyone has called them the twins, instead of Tamara and Theresa, for as long as I can remember. They don't talk much to other people, yet they're constantly whispering to each other. I watch them sometimes and wonder what they say. Their necks arch like two ponies. Their heads almost touch.

Noreen and I got in a scrap at least once a day when we were kids. One time I bit her hand so hard it bled. We don't have many squabbles now, but we're not exactly pals, since she'll be a senior next year and all. She understands a few things, though, and on Thursday when I ask her to drive the five of us to the potholes, she doesn't fight me. Maybe she has plans of her own.

The potholes are three ponds right in a row out west of town. This time of year they're all shrunk up and swampy. Noreen acts as if she doesn't notice we each have a bag, five bottles of sweet wine that Lyla talked her mother's boyfriend into buying. We're not the first ones here. Some boys we recognize are camped out by the small pothole, so we head for the bigger pond, the one in the middle.

My girlfriends have all been drunk before, at least they say they have, but I don't know what to do or how much it takes. We sit in a circle on a rickety dock. In May, the waves would lick at the edge of the wood and the dock would be damp, but tonight the water's nowhere near us. We each have our bottle ready to pass.

They're all different. We have everything from apricot to strawberry. Lyla's mother would strangle her boyfriend if she knew he got wine for us, but he likes Lyla and he's not that old, so he doesn't care about the risk.

If you want to get really high, Lyla tells me, take a good swig each time a bottle comes around. I'm five inches taller than any of my friends, five foot eight and still climbing. We figure it will take more to get me drunk.

I do what she says. The others stop, but I don't quit drinking until all the bottles are lined up in front of me, empty. The twins link arms and start singing a song no one else knows. We ask them. Together they say: It's a drinking song our father sings.

The wine doesn't do a thing to me except slosh in my bloated belly. We can hear the boys from where we sit, loud, ruptured syllables that don't make words. They're older and play football. Lyla's had her eye on one of them since we were in seventh grade, and last year she made me and Meg go to all the high school games with her. Now she goads me into wandering their way, just to say hello. The whole earth tilts when I stand up. I hear myself laugh. It hurts my chest and sounds as if it comes from a well inside my ribs.

I shuffle fifty feet before the wine hits me so hard it sends me reeling, as if I'd smacked head-on into a brick wall I can't see. Everything goes black for a second and returns in a blur. Lyla's pink shirt floats away, like a balloon bobbing ahead of me. She didn't smash up against any wall, only me.

Lyla, I say, I can't go any further.

Come on, she says, keep moving. You're all right.

I have to think, one leg at a time.

The boys are stretched out on their sleeping bags, drinking beers and waiting for the stars to light up.

Well, well, says Lyla's football hero, what have we here?

Wayne Caldwell isn't looking my way, but his friend is, and he sees what's going to happen just in time to get to his knees and break my fall.

Even as I tumble, Lyla forgets me. The boy who catches me holds my shoulders from behind while I puke in the tall grass. I know his name is Tim, but there's no reason for him to know who I am. He hands me something to wipe my mouth, a sock, I think.

I try to stand up, hoping I can get to Meg and the party again, but I can't even crawl by myself and Tim helps me scramble to his sleeping bag. He cradles me in his arms. Lyla sighs. She must be limp as a rag by now. Wayne's kisses are noisy and wet. I know his tongue is in her mouth and she doesn't mind. He grunts, like a pig that's stuck its nose in a corner and doesn't know enough to just back out.

I fall half asleep. Lyla's moans and the boy breathing over her hover at the borders of my dreams. Touch it, he says, his voice airless as an old man's.

I wake with a cramp in my gut, and cuss. Tim jumps to his feet and drags me far enough into the grass to miss his sleeping bag. He wraps one arm around my belly while I heave. With his other hand, he knots my hair to keep it out of my mouth.

The boy with Lyla howls, wild as a rabid dog when the first bullet hits its flank. Lyla doesn't make a sound, no sigh, no moan, no soft whush of a kiss that's almost dry. Her body is rigid. I don't know why I am so sure. She's ten feet away and I can't see her, but in my mind she lies still as a rock at the bottom of a lake.

Meg and the twins stumble around the edge of the pond, staggering toward us in the dark. The twins are arguing. I realize that when I can't see them, their voices sound exactly the same to me. Now I wonder. Maybe they are one person divided up in two bodies and it's all a joke, the way they look so different.

Meg's hand is on my head. She strokes me, rubs my temples. Then she grabs a clump of my hair and gives it a tough yank. It's my last night, she says, some party.

Tamara or Theresa sees the headlights first. She shouts. Meg tells me I'd better get on my feet before my sister finds me this way.

Noreen sees everything. Even though she knows the boys, she doesn't say hello to either one. She's too good for that, a whole year older, and just because Wayne Caldwell played first string quarterback when he was only a sophomore doesn't mean my sister Noreen has to talk to him if she's not in the mood.

We pile in the car. All my friends climb in the back and leave me alone up front with Noreen. Lyla and Meg and the twins are crammed in so tight they can't move. I make out their four faces, round and white as little moons, but I spot only five arms and three bodies, and I think of cattle jammed in a boxcar, the way they all strain their heads toward the open slats, the air. They'll stomp right on top of one another to get a breath, and when the doors slide open to pull cows from the car, there are always more noses than tails.

Noreen looks at me under the murky light of the dome before she slams the door, revs the engine, spins her tires and leaves a billowing wave of dust behind us. I feel the mats in my hair. My knees are muddy from kneeling in the damp weeds; down the front of my shirt there's a crusty trail of spittle. The girls in the backseat barely squeak as we bounce over the dirt road and head for town. All the way home I rock with my arms wrapped around my own stomach and say I'm sorry about a hundred times. My sister wants me to shut up. She doesn't say a word. That's how I can tell. When we get to the house, she takes me straight downstairs. I have to lean on her. I mutter something about my friends and she tells me to forget it. Even though she's older, she's no taller than Lyla or Meg; but she's stronger than any girl I know, and when she clutches me around the waist and I drape one arm over her shoulders, I know there's no chance she'll let me fall.

In the bathroom, Noreen peels off all my clothes,

sits me down in the shower, and turns the water up full blast. Keep your head down, she says. You put your nose in the air and you'll drown, just like a fool chicken in the rain.

She comes for me after a while and bundles me in a towel. I'm safe in bed before Mom and Dad get home from bridge.

I snitch four pills from the cabinet in the bathroom before Lyla and the twins and I walk home with Meg. My head's full of rocks and sticks. They rattle each time my bare feet slap the pavement.

We say good-bye and Meg hops in the car with her two little brothers, her mother, her father. She smiles. She waves. They drive away, just like that. It's all so quick, I don't have time to think.

The four of us sit on the steps of Meg's house with nothing to do. I dig in my pockets for the pills. My mom takes them for her back, or her migraines, or her neck. I can't remember. They take the pain away, she says, but I took one once and it made me feel as if I could climb cliffs all day and never get tired. I figure we can use them now. My friends don't look so good after last night and I suspect it's a lucky thing I don't have to look at myself.

What are those? says Lyla.

Something for hangovers, I say.

We go around to the side of the house and turn on the spigot. Meg's dad forgot his hose. It's flung in the grass, coiled around itself, and the first spurt of water makes it jump and spit. We each pop a fat, green tablet in our mouths when the water runs clear. I turn the water off, almost. No one notices the trickle that dribbles from the mouth of the hose. Let it run all day, I think, all night, maybe tomorrow too. The whole yard will be a swamp. The basement will flood. No one will live in Meg's house for months and months.

Pretty soon, we feel it. We get so calm outside, we glide through the thick air. Inside, we jitter. Our hearts flutter like flapping wings. We want to get going. We don't know where, and everything takes so long; our hands are so slow. We make fun of them, as if they don't belong to us.

It's hot. We don't sweat. Our throats are rough, but we don't need a drink. Our stomachs growl like baby bears, but no one cares about food. That's what the pills do. We feel, but for once, just for once, we don't want anything.

The twins run home to get their bikes. Lyla's bike has a flat, so I tell her she can ride with me. We ride and ride, all the way to the potholes. I pump the pedals, standing up the whole time since Lyla has my seat. All the energy I thought I had is sucked right out of me. As soon as we stop, I collapse in the grass. When I open my eyes, it seems as if a long time has passed, a day and a night and most of another day. The twins have gone home for dinner, and only Lyla's next to me, chomping on a blade of grass, staring at the blank blue face of the sky.

Truth or Dare, I say.

Truth, says Lyla.

I get the idea she wants to tell me about Wayne Caldwell, that she's been waiting to tell me, but I don't ask her, did he touch you, there? Instead I say, did you love Meg?

Lyla props herself up on her elbows, going at that grass in her mouth as if she wants to kill it.

I'll take Dare, she says.

Usually I wouldn't let her squirm her way out of a question, but just this once I say, okay. Then I tell her to kiss me. I tell her I want her to be the boy.

She lies back down, picks more grass, shoves it between her teeth. Finally she says: We start high school in two weeks and I've been thinking, we're getting too old for these games. Know what I mean?

Yeah, I say, I know what you mean.

A bird soars, without beating his wings, so high above us that it can only be an eagle. He starts a dive, then swoops upward again and sails toward the cliffs where he nests. I wonder if his sight betrayed him, if for a second he thought we were something silent and delicious, two wounded rabbits abandoned by the hunter, or if it's only my imagination and he knew all along we were just girls in the grass.

Punishment

ON 1858, THE SLAVE called Lize was hanged in Louisville, Georgia, for the murder of her master's son. I was twelve that day, and now I'm ninety, but I still see her bare feet, scratched and dusty from being dragged down the road. Those feet dangle among leaves so green they writhe like flames. I stand in the garden. The perfume of gardenias makes me dizzy enough to faint.

From where I hang, I see a woman thrown from a ship because her child don' come. She screams too loud and long. The others lift her over the rail, let her fall. They all touch her. They all say: I'm not the one. I see the mother of my mother, standing naked on a beach. The men look her over, burn a mark on her thigh. She squats in a cage for fifteen days. Flies land on her face.

She don' swat them away. I see the bodies chained in the holds of ships. Each man got less room than he got in the grave. They panic, break their own ankles, smother in their own waste. They jump if they get the chance. Black sea swallow a black man. Nobody stop to find him. On the distant shore, I see a runaway stripped of his own skin like a rabbit, torn limb from limb. To teach the others. I see Abe's head. I crawl on my hands and knees, look for his ears. But Walkerman takes them. Did you see how long a man bleeds? Did you see how his head festers in the heat, no way to clean those wounds though I wash him morning and night.

Mama died of a five-day fever we couldn't break with wet towels and ice baths. She left her baby squalling with hunger. That's why Father brought Lize to the house, to keep Seth alive. My brother, four months old, still wrinkled and nearly hairless, was going to have a full-grown woman slave of his own.

Mama would not have abided seeing Lize close to her boy. Father owned more than thirty Negroes, but Mama kept an Irish girl, Martha Parnell, to brush her hair and make her bed, to wipe the vomit off the floor during the weeks when her belly first began to swell, to rock the baby during the days when she lay dying. Mama wouldn't have no nigger woman upstairs, touching her child, fondling the silver-handled mirror on her dresser or cleaning the long, light hair out of her comb. She said they were dirty, first of all, and they had appetites dan-

gerous to men; she didn't want Seth getting used to the
smell of them. Only Beulah, the cook, two hundred and
twenty pounds and fifty-seven years old, was allowed to
stay in the house while Mama was living. And Beulah
was allowed to care for me, to wash the blood from my
scraped knees when I fell in the yard, to lay cool rags on
my head when my temperature flared, to cradle me in
her huge arms when I shook with chills.

Every day, Mama sat for hours listening to me read
from the Bible, making me repeat a verse a dozen times,
until every pause was perfect and every consonant
clipped. She smiled and closed her eyes, her patience
endless: *Again, Selina*. But she couldn't bear my small
wounds or mild afflictions. She had no tolerance for suffering; my whimpering drove her from the room and
made her call for Beulah to come with her root cures.
And I was not permitted to hold the precious mirror or
brush my mama's hair either. She said I was too rough,
too clumsy—seven years' bad luck—I brushed too fast,
only Martha Parnell did it right: *Yes, Martha, that feels
nice*. I hid in the shadows of the doorway. *Yes, like that,
good girl Martha, just another hundred strokes*. Mama's honey
hair caught the light, shot back a thousand sparks of gold
fire. Martha said, "My mam told me the angels have
yellow hair, Missus." She stopped to press the silken
strands to her mouth and nose, forgetting Mama could
see her in the mirror. "Stop that," Mama said, "I don't
have time for such silliness." Martha raised the brush,
gripped it like the stick she'd used to beat the stray dog

in the yard, but she brought it down gently, brushing again—a hundred strokes, just like Mama said—before she coiled that angel hair into two thick braids and pinned them tight, high on Mama's head.

Martha couldn't make Seth take the bottle after Mama died. She was a spinster at twenty, a girl who never ripened, her hips narrow as a boy's and bone-hard, her breasts already shriveled before they'd blossomed. Her body offered no comfort to man or child. Father cursed the sight of her, abused her for the foolish way she cooed at the baby, making him cry harder till he was too hoarse to wail and only squeaked. She dipped her finger in warm milk, but Seth was not fooled. Only Beulah could soothe him, holding him on the great pillow of her lap, quieting him with hands so fat and smooth she seemed to have no bones. She gave him a bit of cloth soaked with sugar water. He suckled and slept. Still, my father's only son was starving; that's what drove him down to the slaves' quarters, looking for Lize.

The man come to the shack. He say, my boy's hungry. He pulls my dress apart at the neck, looks at my breasts like I'm some cow. He say, looks like you got plenty to spare.

Secretly I was glad to hear my father rail at Martha Parnell, calling her a worthless dried-up bit of ground, threatening to send her scrawny ass back to Ireland if she didn't find some way to make herself useful. At my mother's funeral, she tugged on my braids and hissed in my ear, "Looks like you're no better'n me now, Miss Selina. Nothin' but a motherless child with no one but the devil to keep her safe from her daddy. Don't I know. Eight of us. Mama and the ninth dead and me the oldest. Just you watch yourself, little girl, and lock your door at night." My lack of understanding made her laugh out loud. People turned to stare. When Father caught my eye, my face burned, blood rising in my cheeks as if I'd just been slapped.

Martha's only pleasure was bringing sorrow to others. Her lies cost Abe his ears. Mama was nearing her sixth month when it happened. She yelled when a door slammed too hard, fretted when the heat got too heavy— she was a walking misery, despising her own bloated body, its strange new weight, its hard curves. When Martha claimed Abe cuffed her jaw and shoved her down, Mama's judgment was swift and cruel. He was going to be an example. "Can't let these boys get above themselves," she said.

I pleaded for mercy. Martha was always calling Abe, telling him to fetch her some water, fetch her some eggs. One day she'd say, "Help me move this rockin' chair, Abe." And the next day, she'd make him move it back to where it had always been. She ran her fingers through her dry, colorless hair; she batted her stubby eyelashes and never thanked him.

I knew she led him into the grove, looking for mushrooms, she said; but as soon as the trees hid them, she grabbed his wrist and pushed her face against his, mouth wet and open for the kiss he would not give. Scorned gentleman, proper husband of another woman, he knocked the girl to the ground and fled.

Spitting blood from her bitten lip, Martha came complaining to Mama. False and fearful, she whispered she was lucky to have her virtue intact. "Just think what he might'a done if I hadn't kicked him and run."

No one truly believed her, not even Mama, and least of all my father. Still, the orders were given. Three other slaves held Abe down in the barn, and old Walkerman, Father's overseer, took a knife to Abe's head. His howls filled the yard. The green twilight pulsed with the throb of his veins. I sat on the porch, racked by dry sobs. Mama said, "Quit that fussing. It's for your own good. If he thinks he can get away with slapping Martha, maybe he'll go after me next—or you. Slaves must be obedient to their masters on earth, with fear and trembling, just as we are obedient to the Lord," she said. "I want you to find that passage and memorize it for tomorrow's lesson."

Father gave me a swat to the back of the head. He said, "What would people think if they heard you crying over some nigger boy, Selina?"

In the barn, a man lay facedown in his own sticky pool of blood. On the veranda, Father kissed Mother's radiant hair, sat down beside her and laid his hand on her belly. "My son," he said.

"I can't make that promise," Mama told him.

That night I stood at my window and saw my father run toward the grove, a bundle in his arms. His high black boots caught the moonlight, flashed in the dark. I followed him deep in the trees. Limbs snagged my hair; shrubs tore at my dress. I saw the girl-child, naked on the ground, saw him raise the shovel, heard the dull crack, metal on bone, a pumpkin cleaved open to spill the seed. My father dug a shallow grave for my sister. She was small enough to hold in his two broad hands, but he let her drop, unwanted runt, the shoat that will starve because it's weaker than the rest, so you kill it and call yourself merciful.

When I woke, the image hovered between dream and memory. I too prayed my mother's child would be a son.

I saw Abe chopping cotton in the fields, his skin so black it blazed blue at noonday. For weeks he wore a bandage around his head, and I pretended his ears were growing back, that when he unwrapped himself in the evening, he could feel the first nubs, and soon, very soon, the whorls would bloom to full size, firm in the curves and fleshy at the lobes, perfect ears. I touched them in my sleep, peeled away the crust of dried blood, pressed my lips to the fine lines of his scars until they disappeared. I clambered to the edge of sleep to wake hot and tangled in my sheets, my hair damp with sweat, my chest pounding. *Yes, I was the one he hit; yes, I was the one who told.*

*   *   *

After Lize came, my brother ate day and night. He shrieked if she set him down. She couldn't go to the toilet alone or wash her face without bouncing him on one hip. If she tried to talk to Beulah while she nursed, he'd start to whine and then to wail. He needed every inch of her and every breath. Mama hadn't had enough milk for him. After months of hunger, he was determined never to want for anything again. He seemed to know his power already, four-month-old master, king, little man. Green-eyed Lize, flesh-full from cheek to thigh, gave him her body and did not complain.

Lize, I do not believe you loathed my brother. You showed a certain kindness toward him, and fed him well. Soon he grew fat. His fine white hair fell out in patches and the hair that grew in its place was coarse and dark, glossy as my father's hair.

Sounds new to me rose out of the night air. Whippoorwills repeated their own names, a sleepless dirge; the wings of insects clicked and buzzed, a swarm in the yard, hissing in the dirt. Even the earth carried a sound, a distant stamping, a thunderous herd of wild horses.

Abe call at my window. I say, go away. I say, havin' no ears ain't bad enough? You want to die too? But he keep callin' so I go down. He tell me, the boy don' eat. He say, won' take no milk-wet finger. Your own baby gon' die, Lize, and you

22

lettin' some white man's child suck you dry. He cryin' there in the bushes like some fool. I say, what you want me to do? I say, that white boy shake the house with his screamin' if I go. Your baby get one good meal 'fore we all dead.

Later, there were other sounds. One night, before I learned to hide, before I learned to pull the blankets over my head and press my palms against my ears, I heard a muffled cry in the kitchen and crept down the back stairs, shadow of myself.

The man pushed me up on the table. He slap me when I yell. One smack break my nose. Nobody notice bruises on a black-skinned woman, that's what he think. He say, why fight? I never knew no nigger woman who didn't like a white man better'n her own kind. I close my eyes. He don't take too long.

I stood mute, though I saw her skirt bunched up around her waist, and my father's pants dropped to his knees. His black boots were dull and brutal in the dim light, but the pale globes of his buttocks made him ridiculous, a child caught pissing in the woods, his tender flesh exposed.

I remembered my mother's caution, her voice in my skull: *A nigger woman's appetites are dangerous to men.* And I believed, because she spoke to me so rarely. *God is light. In Him there is no darkness.* Still I was afraid, hearing Martha Parnell whisper: *Nothin' but a motherless child with no one but the devil to keep her safe from her daddy.* The son of Noah saw his father drunk and naked and did not turn away. So Ham was cursed, forced to be a slave of slaves to his brothers—because his brothers were good, because his brothers walked backward to their father and covered his nakedness without looking. *Read it again,* Mama said, *slowly Selina, open your vowels.*

The morning I woke with blood on my sheets, I wept half the day, until Beulah came to me, held my hand between her two soft hands, and explained the life of a woman to me. Later she laughed with Lize in the kitchen, shaking over the joke of me, mouth wide, pink tongue clicking: *Silly white girl, cryin' over a bit of blood,* and then, the terrible words again: *Motherless child don' know nothin'.*

Fool or not, I stole a knife from the kitchen, hid it under my pillow, slept with one eye open.

I heard the table scrape across the floor, heard my father cuss. No one was laughing now. I scuttled down to the bottom of my bed and buried myself beneath the heavy blankets. I almost wished to smother, to have him find me there in the morning and repent.

Abe came to me that hot night. I was blue-veined and pale. In the grove, I knelt beside him and touched his dark back, making his muscles mine. I laid my hands on his chest, drained him until my skin was black and he turned white and woman in my hands.

*   *   *

They bury my boy 'fore I know. I go down to the shack. Don'
wake nobody. Don' want to see the husband all weepy eye, ear
place bloody I know 'cause he pick the scabs when he not think-
ing. I find the heap of ground. I dig in the loose dirt. Don' take
me long, he not bury deep. I hold my baby next to my naked
breast. Eat, I say. I wipe the dirt from his eyes, dig it out of his
nose and ears, pull a clot from his mouth. He smell bad and I cry
and cry but I don' make no sound. I say, God, You ain't nothin'
but a dark horse stamping on my soul.

My brother's tiny coffin had flowers enough to drown
him: gardenias and orchids, lilies so white I was afraid to
stare, afraid my gaze would stain them. The gravestone
was twice the size of Seth, its four carved names too great
a burden for a six-month-old boy to bear.

When they come lookin' for me, I don' tell no lies. I say, I
smothered him between my own breasts. He beat and beat at me
with those tiny fists, but I hold him tight till he go limp in my
arms. I hold him tight, then I put him in his basket, rock him
all night.

Lize, I condemned you for the murder of my
brother, execrated you for your bold confession when
lies might have kept you alive. You were dangerous to
men in ways my mother never dreamed. *What fellowship*

has light with darkness? Devil in a woman's shape, you kept me pure, but I thought you deserved to hang, unnatural woman, I'll say it plain: death for death, justice simple and swift.

I never risked my father's curse, never spoke of the ring of bruises on your wrists the day you died or the scratches on my father's face, though I knew well what these signs meant.

At dusk, Abe cut her down, lifted her in his powerful arms as if she weighed no more than a child. Beulah followed, her face a map of sorrow, rivers of blood in the lines of her cheeks, broad forehead a desert to march, bodies laid out in the sun, mountains to rot behind her eyes.

In the shack, the women washed the body in silence, no sound but the wringing of rags and drip of water. They rubbed her until her skin shone, until her feet were beautiful and clean, toes dark as polished stones. They dressed her in white, wrapped her hair in gauze, folded her hands across her chest.

At nightfall the keening of women rose from the shack. Their moans raised Lize up to the arms of God and He took her, begged *her* for forgiveness—poor, betrayed murderer.

The cicadas screamed in the heat of day, the buzz of their wings a wild cry. A constant, rising hum and hiss swelled in waves, a torrent surging through the endless days of summer. In the morning, I'd find their shells belly-up on the steps, a horde that had tried to invade the house each night, and each night failed.

The cotton fields steamed. All day the Negroes chopped, backs stooped, knees bent. All day they coughed, choking on cotton dust. When they stood to clear their lungs, Walkerman cracked his whip, crippled them with a shout. Even the women with bellies bulged enough to burst worked until the sun struck them down and they had to be carried to the shade. Walkerman waved salts under their noses. If they woke, he put them back to chopping until they fell again.

My father festered, grew foul with self-pity. The best part of him, his beloved son, was dead. The sound of his boots on the porch scattered us like mice, sent us all skittering to separate corners of the house. At night, he paced the hallway, and I tossed, gripping the knife whenever his shadow darkened the line of light at the bottom of my closed door.

Martha Parnell still owed Father five years for her passage to America, but in August he sold her time to Walkerman for a single dollar. In the first month, she lost three teeth to his fists, paying at last for Abe's ears. By the fifth month she was swollen up like a spider, her great load teetering on spindly legs. As soon as one child stopped suckling, another began to grow. Her third pushed at her dress when the war started and Walkerman and my father went off to fight.

Walkerman never did come home. Even his body

disappeared, was buried with a dozen others in a common grave or left to rot on the road, bloated and black with worms. Martha was free but had no money and nowhere to go. She stayed long enough to see my father's fields scorched, long enough to see the fine house fill with dust and start to crumble. One day she told me she was going to find Walkerman. I imagined she felt some misguided sense of devotion and wanted the father of her children to have a Christian burial. But I was mistaken. "Have to be sure the bastard's really dead," she told me.

My father lost his legs and his mind in that war. I nursed him for ten years, saw his nakedness daily and could not turn away as the good sons of Noah had. His chest shrank, his eyes fell back in his skull, his hair turned white and fine as a child's. Only his hands were spared. Huge and gnarled, they flailed at the air, cuffed me when I came too near, clutched me in his fits of grief. When he wept, he did not call to Seth or my mother. No, he mourned only for his own legs, kept asking where they were, as if I might know, as if I had hidden them.

Though I knew he could not stand, sometimes I saw him at my bedroom door. His boots gleamed. "Touch me," he wheezed, "I'm cold."

To save what little money I could for train fare to Chicago, I buried him in a four-foot box and marked his grave with a wooden cross. The big man fit in a boy's coffin, and I believed I had nothing left to fear.

I fled the South to take a job as a teacher at a Catholic school. Father would have detested me for that: tasting their bread, drinking their wine, letting it turn to body and blood in my mouth. My constant sins were the lies I told, pretending to be Catholic. Mornings I woke at five to pray. At each station of the cross I murmured: *Hail Mary, full of grace. The Lord is with thee. Blessed art thou among women. And blessed is the fruit of thy womb, Jesus.*

In the chill of those lightless winter mornings, I almost believed in this God who could change Himself to human flesh and die for me. But alone, in my room, the prayers that rose in my heart called out to another god. There were no crosses, only the leafless trees beyond my window.

All these years I have lived in one room, cramped and dim, a place I chose because it did not burden me with spaces to fill. There were no hallways to swarm with drunken soldiers, no parlors to become hospital rooms for the one-armed men, no banisters to polish, no crystal to explode against the wall when my father raged, no trees near enough to scrape the glass with frenzied hands, no scent of gardenia in the spring to make me sick with memory.

Still, there was room enough for my father, withered in my daydreams, spitting gruel back in my face when I tried to feed him, but tall and thick through the chest at night, stamping with impatience, his boots loud as hooves on bare wood. There was room for my brother, his puling cries when he was hungry, and then, his unbearable silence. And there was always room for you, Lize. For seventy-eight years I have watched you hang.

My brother and I were the last of my father's line. Your blood spilled on the ground and flowed like a river to the sea. Ours dried in my veins. You died for my silence. Untouched by a man, unloved by a child, I never mourned the slow death of my body, but now I see this is your just revenge.

All day she sways in the wind, her body light with age. By night she roams the streets. Her bare feet leave no mark in snow. I have seen her often and prayed she would not know me. Tonight, I duck into an alley. Garbage is piled high; the shadows are alive, crawling with rats. Lize follows. She has no age, but I am a fleshless woman, bones in a bag of skin. *Murderer*, she whispers. I am too frail to flee. *I see you watchin' your daddy and me.* She pins me to the wall. *You don' say nothin'.* Her knee jabs my brittle pelvis; the bones of my back feel as if they'll snap. *You kill me, and my child too.* She holds my arms, outstretched. I dangle in her grasp, toes barely touching the ground, legs weak as clay pocked by rain. *You take Abe's ears,* she says, *I can't find them.*

"No, Walkerman tacked them to his wall," I say.

You cry to your mama, tell your lies.

"No, that was Martha."

Whitewoman, you all look the same to me. You all kill us with desire.

I crumple to my knees, alone in the alley. "I never

touched him," I say "only in a dream." The wind whistles down the canyon of brick, repeating Lize's last word. I sob between two garbage cans. The smell is sweet and foul, gardenias rotting in the heat, but I am cold, so cold. I curl into a ball, tight as a fist, small as an ear. The snow is falling. Rats sniff my ankles and scurry away. I am not even food enough for them. Voices hover. Hands stroke my face, hands softer than my mother's hands, fingers tender as Beulah's—Mother never touched me that way. Soon enough the voice is human. The hands shake my shoulder, call me back from the dead.

"Honey, what you doin' in this alley? You lose your way?" The woman's dark face is close to mine, her breath warm with whiskey. "Let Ruthie help you, honey," she says. "Tell Ruthie where you live."

At first I am afraid, Lize. I think it is you in disguise, come back fat as Beulah to torture me again. But no, this woman knows nothing of my crimes. She is condescending and kind. In her eyes I am harmless, my white skin too withered to despise. She helps me find my way home, half carries me up the stairs, sets me in my chair by the window and covers my legs with a blanket. She asks if she can heat some soup, but I say, "No, please go."

From where I hang, I see all the brown-skinned children. You think your death can save them? Your father's blood runs dark in the veins of my children. Your father's blood clots in the heart, bursts in the brain. Your father's blood destroys us all again and again.

"Forgive me," I whisper. The fog of my breath turns to frost on the windowpane. Chill has turned to fever. I cannot kneel or stand, so I sit at my window and wait.

Listen, Lize, I am a desiccated shell of a woman, a cicada you could crush with one step. Put your weight on me, and be done with it. I am old enough and prepared to die.

She does not answer. Her eyes are always open, bulged and blind. She never looks at me. At dusk, Abe comes and cuts her down. I follow her all night, calling her name down unlit alleys. I hear her breath when she stops to rest. But she is a cruel god, she who becomes flesh only to be crucified again and again. At dawn, I am still alive. At dawn, Walkerman ties a noose. Everywhere the silent snow is falling, melting on bare trees until their bark is black and shiny as wet skin. Soon, the men will drag Lize down the road, haul her up, and let her fall. I will see her wrists tied, her blouse torn; I will see her bruised and battered feet. And I will sit, just as I do now, mute witness to her endless death.

The Spanish Boy

Nick and Pauline

Nick's head felt hot and swollen from the tequila. He worked his way slowly through the pack of strangers to find Pauline and tell her he wanted to take a walk by the river to cool off. They'd had another one of their fights before the party and he hoped he wouldn't have to hear any more about it, but he knew he was pretty well in the bag already and his instinct told him it wasn't safe to go near the water alone.

The argument was the same old thing: Pauline was tired of waiting. She'd dropped out of college to work full time so Nick could finish school without getting a job. It was her idea. He was the gifted one. He shouldn't divert his energy. That's what she'd said, but oh boy she sang a different tune these days. Nick said he'd be damned if he was going to settle for a rut of a job in a company where he was sure to be passed over and lost just because Pauline was impatient. What was the big fuss all of a sudden? What were four months when she'd already put it off for two years? He knew she was sick of being a waitress, but no one said she had to stick to that,

33

certainly he didn't. In fact, he wished she'd get out of that place and do something respectable.

They sat on a dock. The air was heavy and the river looked still, as if it had nowhere to go. Nick sprang to his feet and grabbed Pauline's hands, yanking her up with him.

"Let's go swimming," he said.

"You're drunk."

"That will help me stay warm."

"The Charles is filthy."

"That's what they say, but I think it's all a ploy to keep us plain folks from enjoying a midnight dip."

"You don't know how to swim, Nick."

"You do," he said, "like a fish, like a manatee nuzzling the ocean floor." He pulled her close, clutching at her breasts as if they were two life preservers. He whispered fiercely, spitting in her ear, "Say you'll help me, my lovely little manatee."

Pauline was mad at first. She hated it when Nick got buzzed and acted like an idiot. Then she got scared. He had such a grip on her that she couldn't get her breath and she thought he might heave them both into the water before she had a chance to answer and she'd have no choice, because he would certainly sink straight down to the muck at the bottom if she didn't help him. Nick couldn't swim ten feet alone. "I won't," she said, "I won't help you."

He let go of her and crumpled to his knees as if he'd

been puffed full of air and someone had stuck a pin in his behind. "I thought you were my brave girl from the north country," he said, "the girl who climbed mountains, swam across lakes and walked on glaciers. What happened to that girl? Did she die?" This was Nick's favorite way of teasing her, lately, mocking her with these few things that gave her confidence. It was the privilege of love to know precisely how to undermine her best. He paced the dock in long strides, rubbing his chin and pretending to be thinking very hard. "No," he said, "I have it. You lied to me, all those stories." He took great pleasure in this, because he remembered their first trip to the beach, how she had told him about the lake where she swam with her brother; and later, how she had left him wading by the shore while she swam off, away from him, into the dark, cool arms of the waves, and how she had returned, elated, shaking her wet hair on him. He was in love with her then, and they were having such a nice time, he thought, lying in the sun, playing in the sand, but she got hot and bored, and left him for the water.

The memory spurred him on. "You've never even seen a glacier," he said, "much less set foot on one. Admit it, Pauline, you're a pussy like all the rest." He laughed as if this had been a great joke on him, but now he shared it. "Say it, Pauline," he said. "Say, 'I'm a pussy like all the rest.' "

She wouldn't say it and walked away instead, but she felt she had said it, out loud, in front of all their

friends. And she was humiliated, unreasonably humiliated, because she really had greased herself with Vase-
line and had made it the length of the lake with her
brother, three and a half miles. There was no need to lie
about that, no need to create glaciers or exaggerate cliffs.
She had never claimed to be fearless, only to be able to
walk past her fear and do what she wanted to do. But she
didn't want to jump into a polluted river with a man who
was half-cocked and couldn't swim. That was no test of
daring: that was stupidity. The facts made no difference
and Pauline was still ashamed. What he'd said to her had
nothing to do with the Charles or swimming and they
both knew it.

Safe in the crowd of the party, Nick watched Pauline
from across the room. He told himself she was not the
girl he'd met at twenty-one, not the girl who'd inspired
him to drop his high school love practically overnight
and beg Pauline, yes beg her, fall to his knees and plead
with her to go out with him, give him a chance, just
once. It was a bit of a show, dropping to his knees and
all, but he did want her, and he was determined to have
her. She looked like an angel Botticelli would paint, a girl
with round cheeks and pale skin, a girl who rarely
laughed. But she did laugh when he got on his knees and
took her hand and he saw that he'd won.

He conveniently forgot that he had compared the
feet of his last girlfriend to an angel's feet. They were

broad and white, like the feet of angels in the stained-glass windows of his church. He was young enough not to recognize the pattern, or fear it. A woman is an angel only in a man's mind. As soon as he smiles and she returns that smile, as soon as his bare hand touches flesh, she is real, and human, and impure. So when he got on his knees, took Pauline's hand and made her laugh, the end had already begun, but he didn't know it.

Tonight Pauline was dressed in black despite the heat. Her hair was silky and blond and she was tall, two inches taller than Nick. She turned heads. From a distance, Nick could imagine her the way she was, in his memory, but he knew that the skin beneath her eyes was dark and puffy and that the smoothness of baby fat was gone from her cheeks. Her mouth had a tight look from a tendency to absentmindedly clench her jaw. The angel had fled to make way for a woman who was rapidly growing ragged at the edges.

A pantomime began to unfold and Nick was the audience. A man approached Pauline, nodded, cocked his head in question. He stood like a cowboy. She grinned. He pulled her away from the crowd and they started to dance, but the tune was almost over. The next one was slow. Without hesitating or asking, the man wrapped his arms around Pauline. They moved in small circles and she fell against him as if she expected him to carry her away. Nick ducked into the kitchen for another tequila and orange juice. He wanted to feel jealous, but he couldn't muster it, and that's what bothered him most about the way Pauline pressed up so close to the lanky man in tight jeans. Nick was sure she didn't even know him. She was no longer his territory and she was no longer his temptation. Any man could have her, he thought; she was past the point of expecting men to fall to their knees for her.

They didn't talk the whole way home, but it wasn't a sullen silence. Nick acted as if he'd forgotten the whole episode by the river, and the argument before the party. He was in a convincing stupor.

Studying Pauline as she undressed aroused a healthy, belated spurt of jealousy, just the right amount from Nick's point of view, and he said, "So tell me about your cowboy?"

"What do you mean?"

"The guy at the party, with the boots, the one you danced with, cheek to cheek, who was he?"

"How should I know?" she said. Pauline was down to her underwear with her back to Nick. She had a fine backside, he had to admit: high, firm buttocks and a long torso. Her nice ass made up for her small breasts, he'd often said that. She unhooked her bra and slipped a T-shirt over her head before she turned around.

"Well, didn't you ask him his name?"

"Why would I?"

"Oh, no reason. Except I just naturally assumed that after you rubbed up against a guy's crotch it was customary to ask him his name at least. Otherwise the poor fellow might think you don't respect him."

"You can wait all night for a reply to that," she said.

God, she could be aggravating when she used that level tone of voice on him, her mother voice, he called it. It was just as well. He wasn't up for another round tonight anyway, and when she crawled in bed next to him and closed her eyes, he was relieved.

Nick sat in the dark, smoking. A few times he thought he felt her staring at him, but every time he looked at her face, her eyes were still shut and her breathing was slow and even. As soon as the glowing end of one cigarette was snuffed out, he lit another, and in the morning the butts were piled up in the ashtray like the stumps of little dead trees.

The Spanish Boy

Pauline liked to get to the restaurant early enough for a bit of solitude and a cup of coffee or two before the dinner crowd arrived. There were fifty-four red napkins to straighten and fifty-four chairs to check for breadcrumbs or drops of wine that the lunch waiter might have missed. It was the only room she could put in order.

She didn't get much peace this time. As she stood at the window table, she saw her companion waiter for the evening grind out his cigarette, kiss his lover, and cross the street. The lover reminded her of a pony. His hair fell across his face like a forelock and he walked quickly, as if he had to restrain himself from breaking into a canter. From the kitchen she heard a rapid jabbering in Spanish and she knew the cook and the dishwasher had come in the back together.

The kitchen was cramped and sticky. Pauline had to squeeze between the two Spanish boys to get clean silverware. They made her nervous when they talked fast and looked at her. She knew only a few words of Spanish. That was dangerous.

The boys were drinking coffee and didn't move for her. Diego, the dishwasher, put his hands on her thighs as she reached above him. "Want to make a Colombian sandwich, my baby?" He pressed himself up against her, gently, pushing her into the other boy.

"I'm busy," she said. It was a small restaurant and she was the only woman who worked there. The Spanish boys gave her too much attention. They liked her blond hair and fair skin. They talked about her hair as if it were something living, something separate from Pauline.

Diego persisted. "Don't be mean. I love you too much," he said.

"In our language there are two words," she told Diego, "love and lust. They are very different things."

"Oh, no, not to me," he said, "very much the same." He was quite serious and understood her perfectly. That was the problem with Diego. He knew too much. He sensed that she wanted him in some way. When things were good with Nick, Diego left her alone, but when she was unhappy, he smelled it the way an animal smells fear, and he always pounced.

Diego could make every hair on her arms stand on end just by rubbing one finger along the back of her neck, or putting his mouth to her ear and murmuring words that sounded vaguely obscene. His hot breath that close was enough—what he said didn't matter. He knew all her places, but she had no delusions that he cared for her. The boy had instinct, or luck.

She wanted to swat him away. Why did he have to touch her that way and remind her how long it had been since Nick had taken any time with her? Diego had no idea what he was doing, but that didn't make it less cruel. With Nick, she was a block of wood, splintering and dry, and all this boy had to do to bring her back to life was breathe on her. It wasn't right.

Outside, horns beeped. A siren let out a slow howl. Diego massaged the small of Pauline's back with both hands. "You drive me nervous," the boy said.

"Crazy," said Pauline, "the word is crazy."

"Yes," he said, "that too."

"Well you don't drive me nervous or crazy," she said. "I don't feel a thing. I'm not real."

"Don't tease me, my beautiful lady."

She spun around and grabbed his hand, shoving it against her ribs, just below her breast. Yes, that was more like it, more the way she felt with Nick. This little

Spanish boy couldn't get any more out of her, not if she didn't let him. "You want it?" she said. "Go ahead. Touch it." The boy didn't move, didn't even breathe. "Or are you afraid?" I am wood, she thought, with him too, not only with Nick.

Jay, the waiter, had come into the restaurant quietly and was standing in the kitchen doorway, watching. The Spanish boy let his hand drop.

"Just as I thought," said Pauline. "Tell him, Jay. Tell him what kind of woman I am. Tell him to put his hands on me wherever he wants. Tell him I don't care anymore. I don't feel a thing. I'm not a tease. He can touch me."

Jay was confused. He liked the Spanish boys and this didn't look like a game. "She can't feel you, but I can," he said. He made a low curtsy and gave his head a coy toss. "Take me instead," he said. No one laughed. Diego and the Spanish cook pretended not to see him.

Pauline eyed Jay and then Diego, as a mother might glare at her two sons, deciding which to scold first. Diego lowered his head to avoid her. "What's the matter?" said Pauline. "Don't you like me anymore? Don't you want to touch me? I thought you did. My mistake. Weren't you the one grabbing at me just a minute ago? Oh, I see. That was different. That was your idea." She lifted his chin with her fingers, but he jerked free and hissed like a trapped bird. "Of course, why would you want anything

42

I'll let you have? I know your kind. You only have a good time when you make the demands."

She was sputtering. Things had gotten out of hand. Diego's face was blotched with red and the veins of his arms stood out, hard and violet. Jay tried to make Pauline stop, pulling at her elbow and telling her to cool out. She shook him off. She wasn't finished.

"You had your chance," she said. "Don't forget it. If you ever, ever touch me again, I'll knock you across the room. Get it?"

"Enough," Jay said. "We just got customers." He marched into the dining room to greet them.

Pauline faced Diego. She wasn't going to look away first. She was dizzy and her legs were weak. If he slapped her or spit, she knew she'd take it. "*Puta*," he said. It was one of the words she understood.

"I'm not a whore," she said. "I don't do it for money."

"Then for what," he said. He hated her now. She saw it. She thought, desire is only half a step from disgust, always. At least she felt she'd earned it this time. That was something.

She thought of Nick sprawled on her bed like a cat. The morning light filtered through the rice paper shades. It was spring, the first one.

"For love," she said to Diego. Her voice was rough, and even to herself she sounded like a nasty old woman who had never known anything about love. "I do it for love."

43

Pauline and Nick

Pauline overheard a customer say, "She's a swamp hag on her best days." For a split second Pauline thought he meant her and the espressos jiggled and sloshed onto her tray. She glanced at him quickly. He was young and going bald and his shirt was as faded and wrinkled as an old pink pillowcase. A man who was no prize himself could still talk about a woman any way he wanted and no one would think he was a fool. His friend said, "I bet she's not even thirty, but she looks used."

"And used."

"And used."

This made them laugh. Pauline put the espressos in front of them and asked if they wanted dessert. "No, thank you, dear," said the bald one.

She got home around midnight. The lock stuck and she was sure Nick would hear her jangling keys, but she hoped he'd have the good sense to stay in bed and let her struggle. He did. As she tiptoed through the living room, she pictured him lying in bed with his eyes wide open and the thought made her concentrate on every step, like a prowler in her own home.

Lately she'd taken refuge at the restaurant, refuge in the tasks of straightening red napkins and checking silverware for water spots. When she stumbled in at eleven or twelve or one, she was too tired to make love, so it didn't matter that all Nick wanted to do in bed was smoke. The restaurant was safe until tonight with Diego, and now there was nowhere that felt safe.

Usually she couldn't wait to get under the spray of the shower, to scrub away the lingering odor of tomato sauce and grease, but this night she sat in the dark living room for a long time, not doing anything, not even drinking the beer she'd opened for herself.

Finally she got up to go to the bathroom. She peeled off her clothes and left them in a pile on the bathroom floor. She didn't bother to wash her hands or face. In the bedroom, she made no deliberate noise, but she wasn't careful to be quiet, either. She moved as if she were alone in the apartment. Nick was awake. She knew it. He rolled away from her as she slid between the sheets and she thought he probably didn't like the smell of her.

Warm sand, the sound of waves, she tried to think about these things and empty her mind of everything else so she could sleep, but the harder she tried to forget, the more clearly she remembered. *Say it, say, I'm a pussy like all the rest.* First Nick, then Diego. *Puta.* Nick yanked her to her feet. Diego whispered in her ear. Nick said, *you lied to me.* And Diego said, *I love you too much.* White sand almost hot between her toes and the pounding waves so loud they drowned the shouts of children. Diego's hands were on her lower back; his fingers made small circles in the place that always hurt and she felt soothed everywhere when he touched her, from that small hollow at the base of the spine, down her thighs, up through her chest. Her lungs filled with her deep breath. *And used, and used,* her customers said in chorus.

Pauline moved toward Nick, curling her body around his back, kissing his neck, working her way down the knobby bones of his back.

"Didn't you take a shower?" he said.

"No time," she said. She didn't want to talk now. She didn't want to think.

"What do you mean?" he said. "I heard you come in an hour ago."

"Do I repulse you?" she said. "Just tell me if I do." She was taunting him, goading him to say it. He didn't answer and she took his hand in hers and placed it just below her left breast. "Touch it," she said. His hand was rigid and still. She said, "Are you afraid?"

"Don't be stupid."

"Then touch it."

He put his hand over her breast and caressed it thoughtlessly, rolling the nipple between his fingertips.

She climbed on top of him and grabbed his wrists, pulling both his hands toward her breasts.

"Squeeze them," she said, "until you're sure it hurts, then do it harder."

"Are you nuts?" he said. "I don't want to hurt you."

"I want to feel it," she said. "Make me feel it."

He was scared at first, taking her directions. She made him kiss her on one place at the back of the neck near the hairline as if that were the only place that mattered, the only place she could still feel. "No, here," she

46

said, "right here," and she held her finger there until his mouth was on that spot. The must of garlic and her own sweat stung his nose. Only her fingers smelled good, like lemons. She told him to kiss her, to lick her, to bite where he'd just kissed, her nipples, under her arms, the most tender places, her buttocks, her cheek. He began to like the smell. It was all a part of what he was doing, the drug that made him dizzy, the drug that snapped the lock in his brain and made everything all right. He closed his eyes, a free man.

She stood against the wall with her back toward him, touching herself, frenzied, almost clawing. She told him to slap her thighs, inside, up and down, faster, harder, again. He shoved his belt between her teeth and she bit down, tasting leather. His own hand was red and sore; her thighs were redder and still she said: *again, again,* mumbled the word with the belt in her mouth. She flinched, but she never cried out.

Yes, this is what she'd meant all along, now he felt what she'd described when she'd told him about walking on the glacier: every step a question, every step a dare. Was he on solid ice, or was he about to put his full weight on a flimsy bridge of snow? If the snow gives way, there is only the fall, the endless fall, the last thing you do. The crevasse opens its jagged mouth and you are lost.

But he wasn't afraid, not tonight.

Or he was afraid, and he was walking past his fear, yes, like she said.

He dragged her down to the floor and by the time he

47

was moving on top of her he didn't realize her head thumped against the wall with each thrust. She didn't make a sound, no whimper, no grunt, but he couldn't have heard her even if she'd yelled because the water was crashing in his ears and he was swimming against the current with all his might, trying to keep up with her, trying not to lose her.

The waves grew rougher and higher until the last mighty one tossed them both up onto the shore. They clung to each other, gasping for air. He licked the salt from her face, lapped at her skin like a dog, but when he put his mouth on hers, she grabbed a clump of his hair and jerked his head back.

"No, no kisses," she said. And very softly she whispered, "Call me your *puta*. I want you to call me your *puta*."

He would have done anything to please her just then. "*Puta*," he said. It didn't mean a thing to him. He thought it was a love-name and said it over and over, growing desperate with tenderness, but each time he tried to kiss her lips, she turned her head.

Nick

As soon as he woke, Nick reached over to pull Pauline toward him. Now he was afraid, as a man is afraid when he stands on solid earth after he has walked on a glacier. But in that kind of fear, there is strength too.

For the first time he believed he was strong enough to comfort her, strong enough to ask for comfort, but the sheets on her side of the bed were cool; he wondered how long she'd been gone, and why.

Pauline

The morning sun through the high window made a rectangle of light on the kitchen floor. Pauline stared at it without blinking, as if it were a door that had suddenly sprung open and she was just waiting to walk through it.

There was no need to run. She was already free. There could be no more doubt, no more insinuations. Her humiliation was real, a solid thing, not a vague insult delivered in a drunken fight and denied a day later. The marks on her breasts, the small bruises, purple and red where he had sucked and bitten, the soreness between her legs where he had swatted her, these were the signs of pain brought, finally, to the surface. This was no fragile, wounded pride, no aching heart, no tormented soul, just bruises and raw skin and the echo of what he had called her, *puta*, whore, and the memory of what he had done to her body without ever kissing her on the lips, as if she really were a whore.

Yes, this was what she wanted: to bring it all to the surface, make it unretractable, a hurt with a name, a humiliation that could never be justified, not with a hundred words, not with a thousand. It did not matter that

49

she had told him what to do, dared him, commanded him. He had done it. Even if she had known he was lying in bed, thinking about making love to her very slowly, putting his tongue and his wet lips on every place he had bitten, running his fingertips over her thighs and her belly, so lightly, so gently, she wouldn't have cared.

She was going to leave him. The memory of last night would fester for a week, a day, a month, until the proper time, until just the thought of it made her feel degraded and ashamed, until she could throw the fury of her suffering back in his face in a rage of spit and tears.

She thought she had made him prove he hated her, just as she'd forced Diego to show his loathing. A man might try to disguise hatred with desire, like Diego, or with disinterest, like Nick, but she had ripped the veil, torn it away and exposed the raw nerve, the throbbing pulse of malignant love. It was not a veil that could be raised up or sewn together and there was no choice to stay or go: there was only the patch of light on the floor and the open door.

The Sacrifice

*B*EN TRIED TO REMEMBER how the struggle began, but his parents' battle was at least as old as he was, so he could not recall the first bitter word. The fight stirred again as Mama grew fat. An arid wind blew through the house, and their anger dried hard as barren soil in a year of drought.

Mama told Ben she had a present for him: if they were lucky, it might come on Christmas Day, just like baby Jesus.

Daddy said, "Don't be fillin' his head with that nonsense."

Later, alone with his mother, Ben knelt to say his prayers. "Say a special prayer for your daddy," she told him. He squeezed his eyes shut and moved his lips—but could not pray, could not imagine what Mama expected him to ask of God.

She pressed Ben's head against her when he was through, stroking the back of his neck, *my good boy*. Something moved inside her, an animal, a mean little ferret with sharp teeth. He yelped, but she only laughed and pushed his face back down on her hard stomach, forcing him to stay like that until the animal butted its head in her belly again, kicked her with its tiny brutal feet, then curled into harmless sleep.

In the middle of the night, Ben heard his parents' argument swell, or dreamed their torn voices into being. When the years gave him more words, he might claim he heard each accusation, separate and exact, just as one sees the hard edge of a raised knife, even in the dark. But time turns words to clouds, their forms forever changing, blown apart by breath. As a grown man, he might realize he could not have heard what was left unspoken. Still he possessed the knowledge of all children, recognizing the sorrow of his parents as he recognized his own hand. As bone knows its own body and blood its own vein, a child knows his father and mother. The thoughts his parents carried through the house that night clung to the boy's soul, more true than memory, and he would think of them this way:

His father already gray at forty, even his face gray with stubble, pacing the porch, lines of laundry flapping against his shoulders as he stumbled to the rail, his cigarette the only light, hot and red in the damp dark, his father saying: Didn't we move seven hundred miles north to be free of that mumbo jumbo, those swindlers in black who like to keep us scared and ignorant, those moans and chants like chains around our ankles, chains of patience. God rewards those who wait, but three hundred years is long enough.

From the kitchen, his mother answering: And so, this is what you call freedom? Don't I still make my living on my knees? Don't my fingers bleed from putting shirts together from scraps, poking needles through stiff cloth, jabbing myself, sometimes by accident? Tell me how my life has changed.

His father pleading, eyes closed: Your brother wrote to say they were hiring black men to build cars, good jobs, he said. Your sister told you she could walk into any store and try on a dress instead of just holding it up and hoping it would fit. You couldn't pack your bag fast enough, as I recall.

Her voice a rattle like nails thrown across the floor: Who has time to shop, old man? Who has money for a new dress? Does your boy have his own books to bring home from school? Do you drive one of those fancy new cars that roll off the line by the hundreds? Don't talk to me about our better life. Then, softer, barely a whisper, words too jagged to say out loud: What do I have if you take away my hope? This dark room all day. Soot I can't wash off the window ledge. Tiles crumbling on the bathroom floor. My mama and daddy dead, two brothers killed and the other one working for nothing but the fat and the bone, like you, never tasting the meat. My sisters scattered like milkweed in a hot wind: Chicago, Philadelphia, Boston, Detroit—all our days the same, little bits of a better life, a taste of something sweet in your mouth that disappears before you have the chance to suck it. A piece of sugar cane gone stringy from chewing and still you long for the taste, dreaming on it days after it's gone. At least I knew who I was in Savannah. I was barefoot, and the road was dusty, and the sun felt good on my back.

He, almost weeping, crying out to the starless night of fog: Betrayer, betrayer, this was your dream too, this cold northern city of dreams. Didn't we come here to stop loving our misery, to stop praising God for what he would give us—after we were dead, after making us suffer so long, beating us down on earth, three centuries, thirty centuries, hauling ivory, picking tobacco, and I nothing more than a dried-up river in the sun, bloodless man, whipped so hard there was nothing left to whip out of me, so I rose fierce and frail, all bones and skin, but I wouldn't bleed another drop, no sir, not for any white man, not for any white god who gave that man everything he wanted and gave me nothing but a promise: wait wait wait, on the Judgment Day I'll raise you up to sit at my right hand, you my chosen ones, you in golden robes. And you, dark-skinned man, all you have to do is prove your devotion to me. If you have true faith, I'll hear you singing as you walk on your knees, naked for a thousand years.

54

* * *

Daddy mounted the axle. To Ben, this was a miraculous thing. Mama said, "Without your daddy, cars fall apart, break in half first pothole they meet." Ben couldn't remember Georgia, but he knew his father was a janitor there. Mounting an axle sounded like a special job, a man's job, not like sweeping—which any woman and even a child like himself could do.

He told the boys at school about his father's important work and they laughed at him. "Your daddy stand in one place all day and rivet one pin, just like my daddy," Henry Clay said. "He miss one, nobody mind." Henry Clay was two years older and a head taller than any other boy in the fifth grade. Words on the page meant nothing to him, but he knew plenty about any topic you might name. The boys said Henry Clay talked truth and nothing but. His ears were too big and stuck out straight from his head. His hair was shaved so close to the skin his skull gleamed. Ben heard his mama was white and never left the house. Then he heard she was only half white and ran away. Either way, Henry Clay got somebody's fine golden skin, and the girls at school giggled when they passed him, called him "pretty boy" behind his back, and never seemed to notice those ears.

Ben didn't tell his mother what Henry Clay had said. No harm in her believing Daddy's hand kept every car in Detroit on the road. He thought of his father, the cars rolling past day after day . . . all the cars the same and that one pin shining up at him like an eye, a terrible blind eye staring at him as he tightened it, tool quivering in his hand, a burst of energy, the frenzy of electricity buzzing from his fingers to his shoulder, then dying flat, his job done—done, until the next stripped frame stopped in front of him, until another steel eye mocked him, and the tool sprang to life.

In the evening, Daddy sat downstairs on the front steps, talking to anyone who passed. He drank three beers, never more or less, and smoked two cigarettes. Mama scolded him even for that, calling alcohol and tobacco the devil's drugs, "bad as burning money," she said, using the same words nightly, as if they'd come to her for the first time. Father rarely talked back now that Mama's thighs were so thick she couldn't cross her legs, now that the fat of her arms flapped like empty pockets. She had a power on account of her superior size, so he didn't bother to argue a point, no, didn't even grunt— but he didn't go to church either, and didn't stop buying beer or rolling smokes.

Aunt Eveline came from Chicago to help Mama in her last weeks. She'd had three husbands and none were dead, but all had suffered. She was copper-skinned and tall, beautiful in the way Ben's mother used to be before she puffed up, grew an extra roll of flesh under her chin and got squinty in the eyes.

Ben watched Aunt Eveline's big calves as she strutted across the living room in her high heels; the knots of muscles bulged hard and her gold rings flashed as she smoothed her dress over her round little belly. Mama said, "Eveline, they cut that dress to your shape and sewed it on like skin, I swear." Daddy went into a coughing fit and left the room, choking.

Eveline's coat had fur around the collar, and she let Ben touch it, lose his fingers in it, rub it to his cheek; and it felt so good until his aunt threw back her head and laughed, saying, "That boy of yours is gonna be a fine lover, Maggie. He likes the feel of things." Mama told her to hush up, he was a good boy. So Ben knew there was something bad in him, something Aunt Eveline saw right away and Mama denied, something to do with the way he stroked her fur collar. He swore he would never touch it again. But he did touch it, that forbidden thing. When he was sure everyone else had gone to sleep, he crawled into the closet where the smell of damp wool was strong enough to smother him. His blind fingers probed until he found Aunt Eveline's coat and pulled it off the hanger, caressing the soft, cool fur in the dark.

Daddy said Aunt Eveline had tried to kill each of her husbands in turn. Uncle Harry ate some kind of slow poison for weeks before he caught on. Uncle Slate got shot in the hand and said it was a mistake: she didn't know the gun was loaded. She said it was a mistake all right; she was aiming for his chest and didn't know she was such a bad shot. Uncle Winston claimed she lured him into the bathtub one day and tried to drown him. This was her way of letting a man know she was tired of him. Since no husband in his right mind would give up a fine chunk of woman like Aunt Eveline, she had to take strong measures. Even so she complained her ex-husbands had a way of hanging on, showing up on Sundays, tipping their hats and asking if she might spare some of her lemonade.

Legally she was still married to Harry Dean Dennison, which made her marriages to Slate and Winston nonbinding, but she said she married Harry down in Georgia when she was a mere child. "Georgia's another country," she said. "I'm from Chicago now. Anything I did in that other life is a lie, something that happened to a different girl, a skinny black girl with nappy hair and faded dresses. Look at me, am I that child?"

She twirled, her bright dress floating above her knees, her buttocks high and firm, her red hair nearly straight. Everyone had to agree she was not that girl.

On Wednesday night, Mama took Ben to a prayer meeting. His daddy stayed home with Eveline. Ice glazed the sidewalks, and Mama had a hard time balancing her belly. She clung to Ben. He knew if she went down he wouldn't have the strength to get her back on her feet, so he was relieved when the thin yellow woman who lived next door offered to walk them home.

Ben busted through the door first, while Mama did her cheek kissing and good nights with the neighbor lady. He found Eveline and his father tangled together on the couch. They sprang apart, but there was no hiding the fact that Eveline's dress was tugged off her shoulder, one breast pulled over the top. She tried to tuck the thing back in, but it wouldn't go, and she scurried from the room, her breast flopping.

Mama breathed heavy on the stairs, climbed slow and flat-footed, her load an aching burden, her hand always on her back now. Ben stared at his father's face, at the mouth and cheeks smeared scarlet from Aunt Eveline's lipstick. Daddy kept rubbing his hands on his pant legs, trying to wipe away what he'd done. He made it to the bathroom just as Mama appeared in the doorway, a huge black shape silhouetted by the light on the landing.

Aunt Eveline packed her bags and took the train back to Chicago the next day. Mama shook her head and said, "Isn't that just like Eveline to come all the way out here to help me with the new baby, then up and leave when I need her most."

Right to the last days, Mama kept on going to church even though everyone advised her to sit still with her feet up till her water broke. She took none of their advice. She wouldn't even let *him* spoil it with his mumbo jumbo talk, his refusal to put on his blue suit, his stubborn Sunday sleep. He could do as he chose, but the boy was hers and the baby was hers, and they were going to know God and his mercy; they were going to see what happened to a man who didn't believe in mercy, their own father, a man who turned to other comforts, earthly comforts, a man who shriveled up inside. She had to be strong because she loved that man once, but this was God's plan to show her children, to show her, what happened if you tried to live outside grace. Some folks dreaded the Judgment Day, but she longed for it, that day when men's fortunes would be reversed, that day when neither the rich nor the poor had anything to buy or anything to own, and the naked would be judged only by their souls.

Ben arched toward the choir. The men sang out a line and the women hummed it back, an echo in the canyon of the heart. The congregation moaned, a deep suffering sound, a pack of starving wolves trapped in the woods of a winter dusk. His mother stood, hands raised above her head, loose skin of her arms shaking, huge belly rocking. He was afraid of this woman, this stranger, her eyes screwed shut, her mouth opened wide as it would go, so anyone who looked could see her big pink tongue, her broken teeth. Women fanned themselves and some fainted and had to be carried away, to a secret place in the back of the church where something vile and strong was waved under their noses until they woke and wept and said they'd seen Jesus.

The preacher rose in his pulpit, shouting: "Doesn't God test the children He loves best? We must have faith even in our despair. What is faith to a rich and happy man?"

The congregation, having only one mind, answered: *Nothing, nothing.*

"So praise the Lord when you suffer."
I do.

"Praise the Lord if He asks you to show your love when your stomach's empty and your feet are tired. He asks for nothing compared with what He gives. See how He tested the good man Job."

Poor Job.

"No, *fortunate* Job to be strong enough to prove his faith. Didn't he bear more affliction than you or I and still love God?"

Patient Job.

"And didn't God test Abraham, the one who could talk to God, who said, 'Listen, Lord, there might be a righteous man in Sodom.' God heeded the words of Abraham, and the righteous were saved from destruction."

The Lord is merciful.

"Still God tested Abraham and said, 'I want you to take your son Isaac, your best-loved child, to the mountaintop and offer him there as a sacrifice to me.' So Abraham took his son; he took the fire and the knife, just as God asked."

Yes, he did.

"Isaac said, 'Kill me, Father, if God asks for my life, but be swift.' As the father raised the knife, God's angel came, and the child was spared. A ram appeared, snared in the brambles. The angel said, 'Abraham, kill this ram for God instead.' "

Praise God.

"Is God cruel to test us?"

No, God is great.

"Isaac might have been killed by the hand of his own father."

No, God has mercy.

"How can God ask a man to sacrifice his own son?"

God gave his only son.

"So that we might be redeemed."

To save us from sin.

Ben couldn't blink. His mother had to unpeel his fingers from the cloth of her dress. He was in the woods, alone with his father, hunting squirrel and rabbit, alone with Daddy and the rifle. What would his father do if God asked? No, Daddy wasn't like that. Daddy didn't believe and wasn't saved, even Mama said so. But just suppose God spoke to him directly. What would he do then?

Mama slapped him, not too hard, just a smack to the side of his head to bring him out of the forest. She said, "Stand up, Ben, preacher's passin'." He stood and saw the preacher floating down the aisle, his violet robe billowing out behind him, a blue robe glowing red underneath, a blue robe soaked with blood, turning violet. The preacher did not feel the blood running down his arms, did not see the dark trail he left on the floor.

A choir boy in white followed the preacher. He was long in the limbs and narrow. His hands had grown before their time and hung from his bony wrists, awkward and strange; but when this boy raised his voice, the song was high and clear, an angel's call, so sweet Ben thought it would shatter his heart; his glass heart would explode, and still the notes would climb, higher and higher until he couldn't hear them with his ears: he could only feel them in his body, in the air, the whole world vibrating around him, his bones humming.

The stained-glass window shimmered in the morning light. Jesus stood with a lamb under one arm. He smiled. *I am the lamb of God,* he said to Ben. *I will be slaughtered.* The words buzzed in Ben's head though he did not think them, did not want them, and he stared at the feet of Jesus, beautiful and pale, each toe full and round; Jesus had long feet that made Ben want to fall to his knees and wash them with a cool rag, made him want to trick God and kill a ram instead of Jesus. He would hide with Jesus in the hills and wash the feet of Jesus in the streams.

They were all singing now, singing about the river with milk and honey waiting on the other side. Their voices surged: *deep and wide;* he couldn't swim, and the sound was honey, thick and sweet, lapping over his face, in his nose and in his mouth.

Ben's mother lay in bed, rubbing the great loaf of her body, listening to the slow breathing of the man beside her. She tried to stop up her thoughts, to keep from saying: *God does ask for our sons.* But she saw black boys hanging from the trees, the dark blossoms of a Southern dawn. One brother came home and one never did, both dead. Milo, back from the war and proud, a fighting man who knew how to use a gun, how to give orders and get the job done. And they expected him to sit quiet at the back of the bus, to shuffle on by, yes'm to death; and when they took him, they said he looked a white woman in the eye. Milo, the one she saw, they killed twice, shot and dragged a mile before he was hanged, the rope cut up and sold in pieces for souvenirs. Walter just disappeared, but you don't have to pull a body from Ogeechee Creek to know where it is, to see it bob to the surface of your dreams, naked and bloated, turned blacker than any black man, and still your brother.

Hoping, she was hoping this child would be a girl— God rarely asked a woman to give her girl-child back to him.

She told herself, God gave his only son, and some of our sons live. She guessed that was the difference, but her mama had to give up two sons, so even if Joe Willy lived and moved to Detroit, didn't her mother still give up twice as much as God? It was a bad thought. She wanted to strangle it, but she felt she was strangling her own mama's memory and she couldn't stand watching Miss Retta die a second time. *God has a plan we can't see,* she said to her mama, but she knew the old woman didn't believe her.

That baby took her own sweet time, waiting for the coldest day in January to wail her way into the world. Ben's mother stopped going to church for a while because she couldn't bear to be away from Mona Lee even that long.

Ben knew that Mama loved the baby more than she loved him. She held it to her naked breasts and didn't mind who watched. And it—that squirming, wrinkled thing—what was so special about a red baby who only squeaked when she wasn't crying, stupid as a rabbit scrambling for a teat, who could yell like picks were being poked into the soles of her feet, then stop as soon as Mama gave her the nipple, all gurgles and smiles when she had what she wanted, selfish thing. She couldn't even turn over by herself or look you in the eye, so why did Mama love her best?

Daddy knew his misery and called him "my big boy," saying, "The baby needs your mama now and no one else can take her place." He told Ben, "She was that way with you too, but you don't remember. Hardly let me touch you in the beginning." But Ben didn't believe him because how could anyone forget the smell of his mama's milk when nothing, nothing could ever be so sweet?

Ben's mother heard Miss Retta say: *Don't love one too much 'cause God will take him away.* The old woman stood in front of Maggie: hunched and gray; papery skin creased and dry, hanging off brittle bone; eyes yellowed, nearly blind; twenty years older than the day she'd said it. "Get out of here, old woman," Maggie said. But the dead just laugh at the orders of the living. Still Maggie persisted. "That's how slaves think. Long as you think that way, you're no more free than your own granny." *I'm not free*, Miss Retta said, unashamed. "God's not the man, Mama. He don't own you that way. He don't take your babies just to punish you." *Milo and Walter, your two who lived less than an hour, my own daddy laid on the tracks—shall I stand here all day and name the dead? Don't love one too much, Maggie.*

Maggie stood at the window, pressing Mona Lee to her chest so tight the baby woke screaming. In the glare from the glass, Maggie's mother disappeared, but her words hung in the room, foul as rotten meat. After Ben, God did take back two in a row, both born before their time, the first one dead, the second strong enough to struggle for an hour and die in her arms.

After that, she couldn't bear to let Nathan touch her—not that way. He curled around her in bed, spooned her, his belly hugged up close to the curve of her rump. He held her all night and never complained, though she could feel him hard against her and it made her ache to keep herself from him, a dull throb from her chest to her thighs, not desire but the lack of it. She saw what it did to him, this keeping to herself.

But she did. All those years.

And then one night she turned toward him, and he was ready. She thought she was too, but she was parched and he tore inside her; still she let him because she

66

wanted something else, and now there was Mona Lee, her precious one. She believed the soul of one of her dead babies had another chance to come into the world. So God was merciful. He had raised her child just as he'd raised his own son.

Still she was afraid, and she went to Mona's crib at night, even when the baby didn't cry, more fearful of her silences than her howls. For a month, she couldn't leave the house without the child—even when Nathan and Ben were there to watch her, even though shopping would be easier without a baby strapped to her back. She told herself caution wasn't unnatural, but she was glad that her mother didn't come to her window again.

Ben's father said, "Pretty soon you'll know more than your daddy." He was thinking how he'd swept the floors of the school where his son wasn't welcome, emptied wastepaper baskets in a library where he couldn't sit down. "I never did finish the fifth grade. Got a job selling newspapers."

Ben said, "I can get a job."

Mama and Daddy had a good laugh over that, and Mama said, "No, baby, boys smart as you do best to stay in school. You can be anything if you're educated—a doctor, a lawyer—mayor of Detroit." Ben couldn't imagine any of that. No one he knew had those kinds of jobs. They were only words. He wanted to mount axles, just like Daddy, even if Henry Clay was right about his father just riveting one lousy pin.

He wanted to know what Daddy knew. His father could skin a squirrel in a minute; he had some secret understanding of how skin connects to flesh, so his knife was fast and made no false strokes.

Ben longed for his father's fine fingers, and the patience to bend over a table for hours as his father did, turning string and feathers and bits of scraps to beautiful flies, golden and green-headed, some black with red wings, some so pale they took on the color of water or sky. His flies were magic, but he never used them himself, having no taste for fish. He sold them all for pennies and dimes, except the one Ben stole and kept in a tiny box stuffed deep in his drawer, one with a glistening purple body and four clear wings, too delicate to touch.

Yes, Daddy had magic in his hands, even if he did just rivet that one pin.

His father said, "Read something to your daddy, makes me happy to hear you read." He watched himself in the library, running his fingertips down the spines of the books, afraid he'd be caught and lose his job if he dared to lift one off the shelf. The fresh pain surprised him; that library was years in the past, hundreds of miles south.

The only book in the house was the Bible. Ben couldn't refuse, but he was afraid to open those pages, afraid of the stories hidden there. He turned to the psalms. They were only songs, safe if you spoke them, safe if the choir boy didn't raise his sweet voice. He read:

"Be merciful to me, O God,
be merciful to me,
for in thee my soul takes refuge;
in the shadow of thy wings I will take refuge. . . ."

His father grinned. He said to Mama, "Like music,"
and wanted to ask: "Who needs church, all that hollerin'
and whoopin' when God is right here in this room? God's
got a fine pair of ears. He don't need all that screechin' to
hear you call. Listen. This child talks to God." He
wanted to tell her that to free her, but she was already
rocking and crooning to the beat of Ben's voice, and he
could see she was longing to be cut loose, so what good
was there in saying, "Hush now, let God hear you whisper."

Maggie thought Nathan might still be saved, the
way he beamed when the boy read those holy verses. She
would have liked to say that was the reason she began to
feel tender toward him again, but when she was honest,
when she traced it back, she realized it had something to
do with Eveline's visit. Maybe it was her sister's heat in
the house, or maybe it was what Eveline said, defending
herself for the way she treated her men: "Better to shoot
a man dead than strangle him slow like you're doin' to
Nathan."

Henry Clay shot staples into his hand until his palm was
dotted with droplets of dark blood. He ate paste and
carried a knife in his pocket. Being kind enough to ex-

plain the true nature of the work Ben's father did, he also took it upon himself to explain to Ben how his mother could be pregnant again so soon after Mona Lee was born. He told Ben how his daddy climbed on top of Mama and what he did, and he said, "Haven't you heard your mama cry out in the night like she's being beat or stabbed?" Ben thought, *No, Mama only cries in church*, but then he started listening and there were sounds, sounds he didn't like, low sounds in the throat, his father grunting, and high sounds from Mama, not at all like her moans in church. Ben thought, *How could he?* And why did Mama let him when she'd swelled up so big she didn't have to do anything she didn't want for anybody?

When he couldn't bear the night sounds, he covered his head with his pillow, but it was always too late because his parents' voices rang in his skull. He imagined his father on top of her—he, getting smaller by the second, shrinking until he was no bigger than a boy, no bigger than Ben, and Mama blowing up with laughter, puffing up fatter and fatter. Daddy squirmed on top of her, clutching at her breasts, trying not to fall between her huge thighs where he would be swallowed, forever lost.

But the next morning, Daddy was his usual size. And the next night, when Mama was giving Mona Lee her breast, Daddy had that look like he was warm all over. His skin turned almost red, beads of sweat pearled on his forehead and under his nose. Then he moved his hands under the hem of Mama's dress and touched her knees, so lightly, just with the tips of his fingers.

Ben's mother planned to go back to doing housework as soon as Mona Lee would take the bottle from the woman next door, but she couldn't now that she was pregnant again. Who wanted a maid who could bend over only halfway? Who wanted a cleaning woman who couldn't get down on her hands and knees to scrub? But the money she'd stashed under a loose plank was gone, so she started taking in laundry for some of the ladies she knew on the other side of town. On Saturdays, Ben's father drove her from house to house along the shore of Lake St. Clair to deliver perfect folded piles, and haul away lumpy bags of soiled clothes.

All day, every day, there was washing, mending and ironing, and still there was a day's work left at the end: her own house to clean, her family's dinner to cook.

Ben was amazed by the houses where these people lived. He lived on the second story of a row house where there was always laundry strung up across the porch, noisy flags in the wind. The houses he saw on Saturdays were big enough for four families, clean and white, their sloping lawns green, their driveways long and shaded, each house tucked in a private wood. Even in the dense days of summer, there was a breeze here off the water and dappled shadow, places to lie down and sleep underneath trees. He was glad to leave the grit and steam of their own house, glad to leave the stale air of his treeless block where the grass burned hard and yellow and the buildings blistered in the heat, where a few scabby bushes clung to spent soil. If one of the older boys busted open a fire hydrant, they had some relief.

Ben and his daddy sat with Mona Lee in the car while Mama went around to the back doors of the big houses. Ben never saw the ladies who lived here, but he saw the fine clothes Mama brought home, the silky camisoles, the linen skirts, and he saw the pale children. One tall, fat boy with curly yellow hair stared at Ben through the window of the car until Ben made a face, putting his thumbs in his mouth and stretching it as wide as he could, using his fingers to push his ears forward and flap them back and forth.

The boy ran away and Ben was proud, thinking he'd scared him off, but he returned with two smaller boys and a toddling girl. They pointed and laughed, mouthing the words, *Do it again, do it again.* And he did, hating himself. The boys howled, but the freckled girl stood stunned, then burst in tears. The whole time, Ben's father did nothing except grip the steering wheel, staring straight ahead.

In the dead of July, when the air was too thick to breathe and your own skin was too much to wear, Mama's church had revival meetings every night for a whole week. She left Mona at home, thinking God wouldn't dare let any harm come to her during the revival. Many learned to love Jesus out of nothing but weariness, realizing the heat was easier to bear if you gave up your soul without a fight.

Ben saw the stained-glass window waver as if it was underwater. The beautiful white feet of Jesus glowed, and for the first time Ben wondered if God was white too. He thought that might explain what the preacher said about black folks having to suffer here on earth, but he began to wonder if this white god was really going to reward them in his heaven, or if white people would still live in all the big, cool houses on the lake.

His mother was rocking and humming, a low sad sound, sorrow turned to song and set free. She couldn't listen to the preacher anymore. She couldn't bear to think too much about the words. She tried too hard to give them sense, but there was no sense. There was only God's plan. Who was she to question? *Nobody.* She couldn't ask, she could only wait. But when she closed her eyes, she saw her mother keening at the sun on that sweltering day when they brought Milo home in a sheet black with blood. *God doesn't ask for any more from you than he asks of himself. Too much. And what does death mean to God anyway? Don't think about Mama, don't think about Milo and Walter.*

Her voice split like a ripe melon cleaved open and she was free of thought and floating on the waves of her own dirge; someone sang back to her, wordless and sweet, an angel answering her own thoughts. Then there were hands on her, pressing, pressing, holding her down, pushing her head below the surface until she screamed and the waters parted. Tears trickled into her ears because she was pinned flat to the floor. She heard her own story, the story of all women, running through her veins like a river, a river of women's blood, rolling over the stones that had beaten them dumb. This story could not be written, only known, a bloom in the brain, a seed in the hull of her heart, her mother's hand on her cheek in the heat of a fever, all the hands of women who had washed the feet of the dead without weeping. These were the hands that touched her now, from the inside.

Ben watched his mother jerk on the floor in the aisle. Men reborn held her down with their merciful hands, but even five were not enough. She bucked and shouted and didn't stop until the skinny yellow woman who lived next door knelt beside her to whisper something in her ear, kissed her forehead and smoothed her damp hair. Only then did Ben's mother open her eyes. The woman tore the men's hands from his mama's arms, and Mama said, "I heard an angel singing in my voice." The yellow woman said, "Course you did, honey."

On the way home, Ben asked, "Is God white, Mama?"

"God ain't got no color, baby. You know that."

"Then why—"

She smacked his mouth with the backside of her hand, knowing his question before it was half said. "Don't you ever ask for explanations like that from God,"

74

she said. "God don't have time to waste talkin' nonsense to ignorant boys."

He hated her then, and God too, and he wanted to run away where God couldn't find him or ask terrible things of him. He wasn't going to take that white Jesus with him either, that Jesus could take care of himself, and if he wanted to die for his father, he was welcome to it, but Ben wasn't going to have any part of it.

On the last night of the revival, Daddy said it was going to warp Ben's mind to go there night after night; it was unhealthy and too damn hot to be sitting in church smashed up against all those people. Mama said, "Don't you swear in front of me," and dragged Ben out the door.

Ben was glad his father refused to come to church, glad he wasn't there to see how Ben made Mama ache. The preacher called the unclean ones. "Let all sinners be saved," he said, and the congregation shouted: *Hallelujah*, loud enough to reveal the night sky, violet and endless. Stars stabbed the darkness like the needles of fire that pricked Ben's skull and spine, working their way into his buttocks and thighs, stinging his palms and the back of his knees, finally piercing the soles of his feet.

He was afraid as he had never been afraid because he knew if he was saved, then he was bound to do whatever God asked. If the knife was raised, he'd have to lie down.

Mama wept beside him. *Oh yes, dear Lord, let my child be saved.* And the preacher kept calling: "Oh you who still drift in the seas of sorrow, come now and accept Jesus as your savior." Mama nudged him but he didn't move. He didn't want to be saved. He didn't want Jesus to die for him, not sweet baby Jesus, not the Jesus with the beautiful white feet in the stained-glass window.

Little girls in pale dresses and patent leather shoes sobbed as they walked up the aisle, clutching tiny purses in gloved hands. Ben stared at their brown legs and white ankle socks, but he could not follow.

The preacher said, "Jesus loves you." And the girls were blessed and they got to stand there in the front of the church, where everyone could see them, and everyone would know they were saved. Ben almost believed he saw a light glowing around their heads; they were washed in that light till their skin shone bright and pale, but he, he was dark and miserable, shrinking into himself, melting, hot as tar.

Now the boys came too, one by one, boys who had begun to grow so fast that their pants were inches above their ankles, and younger boys who still waited to spurt and wore their cousins' hand-me-downs, two sizes too big, bagging in the butt, cinched tight and gathered by a belt high on the waist. Even Henry Clay marched forward, head high, eyes full of light, Henry Clay, who in his real life was expert on the way of married folk in the night, Henry Clay who left live things in the teacher's desk, things with hairless tails or scaly backs, and who peeked under the dresses of little girls who skipped rope, this Henry Clay was going to be saved.

Mama wailed now, "Oh my baby, please don't make me wait." She would have suffered less if Ben had pummeled her with his little fists, battered her on the outside instead of pinching at her heart, leaving her to imagine being called on Judgment Day, rising into Heaven, where she could see her husband and her son lying dead on the ground, their bodies foul, their eyes plucked out of their skulls.

The preacher said, "The good Lord won't rest tonight if we leave one suffering soul in danger." Everyone knew Ben's soul might burst into flame before their eyes. Folks were dizzy from breathing too hard and getting too little, so they all pleaded, but they could not make him rise, even when the women close enough to touch him lay hands on his head and his knees, his arms and the sharp wings of his shoulder blades.

Only he would understand why he had to keep his heart away from Jesus, this Jesus he had loved and had wanted to rescue from God, this white Jesus who cared so little for the shriveled soul of one small black boy in Detroit that he could not even answer his questions. He felt his blood pound against the back of his eyes when the preacher touched the cheeks of the saved children and said Jesus was waiting to take their hands.

He wanted to promise Jesus he would find him later, would wash his feet and bind them with heavy muslin, but he knew he would be lost if he weakened for an instant. When he broke, when the tears flowed and he fell to his knees, everyone around him praised the Lord,

77

thinking this boy who would not get up for Jesus had
been truly saved, taken with so much force it sent a
tremor to his bones and left him too limp to stand. They
did not guess that he wept with the knowledge of his own
fate, seeing the sand of the scorched earth blowing over
his withered body, burying his hands, filling his eyeholes
and gaping mouth.

Now the chants shook the ground and the floor split;
a great crevasse cracked open with a rumble louder than
all thunder. He had to grab his mama's big leg; she was
about to step in the chasm and fall away from him forever, but he caught her just in time to hold her tight, to
be crushed against her soft breasts, to breathe the smell
of milk gone sour in the heat, and then to barely breathe
at all. The crevasse closed and the floor lay flat and still,
unscarred but somehow terrible. They were safe. Mama
pressed her arms against his ears and the chants became
nothing more than the endless murmurs of bees.

Somewhere a door opened. The night was cool. A
breeze whipped his back and sizzled like water putting
out a flame.

At home he longed to cry but only stared at the
wall, praying that Jesus would forgive him, though he
could not forgive Jesus for showing him his perfect feet
and then walking away.

He heard Mama singing in the bathroom and was
afraid she might come to his room and touch his sweaty
back. But she was too tired to bother with him again

tonight. All he felt was the sodden rag of his soul being wrung out between two powerful hands.

On Saturday, Daddy took his rifle from the closet and said he had a craving for squirrel. Mama bounced fat Mona Lee on her thigh. She said, "Take Ben with you," and Ben knew she wanted him out of the house so she could be alone with the baby.

Daddy wiped the long silver barrel with an oiled rag. It caught a flicker of light from the window and shot back a bar of brilliant white fire. Ben didn't want to be alone with his father in the woods, especially when Daddy slapped him on the back and said, "Let's go, son."

They drove north and hiked into the hills, where there were no fences and no paths. Sun glinted through trees, and Ben kept feeling someone behind them; but every time he turned, he saw nothing but shadow and leaves shaken by wind. Ben wanted to call out: *You can follow us, but I won't help you.*

The blast of the gun shattered the air and Ben waited for pieces of the broken blue sky to fall on his head. His father yelled, "I got one," and Ben felt the heat of a bullet tear from his chest to his spine. His father fired four more shots before they left the woods. Each time the gun seemed to explode in Ben's own body, ripping muscle, splintering bone, but still he stumbled after his father, and the other one stumbled behind him, his bare feet cut and bleeding, each step leaving a dark footprint in the dirt.

His father lifted the squirrels by their necks, holding them up for Ben to see, grinning, proud. Ben watched their feet dangle, glad for their small deaths because each one made him more safe. The last one was fatter than the rest. His father said, "She's a fine one," and he was satisfied to kill three and miss two.

The one who followed breathed harder as night crept through the trees. It was a long walk back to the car, but they stopped by a trickle of a stream to gut the squirrels, "So they won't poison themselves," Daddy said.

He skinned them first and they were more naked than a man could ever be, their wet flesh brilliant even in the thin light of dusk. Ben couldn't watch him gut the first one, but then he leaned over his father to glimpse what was inside, wondering if he looked that way, a tangled rope of bowel, a small and pitiful heart.

Daddy did the big one last, whistling through his teeth. "I like the fat ones," he said. Now Ben looked at her eyes, black and moist, still so close to living that she seemed to know what they did to her, seemed to watch his father pull back the ribs with his strong thumb to take out the heart and lungs.

When they stood up, the man hiding in the trees did not rise to follow them but stayed behind, curled in the dark crook of an oak, licking his wounded feet. Ben longed to run back to him, but it was too late, too late for sacrifice or salvation. He would not be followed in these woods again.

In the car, he hung his head out the window and let the wind beat his face until his eyes teared and stung. He thought he heard his father say, "Best not to tell your mama."

Mama had the vegetables ready and went to work making squirrel stew. Ben looked at her swollen stomach and felt so sick he had to lay his head down on the table. His father stood behind Mama and kept trying to put his hands on her belly. She batted him away, laughing, but finally she turned to kiss his nose and squeeze his butt. *How could she*, Ben thought, *after what he done.*

Alone on his bed, Ben opened the box where he kept the fly his father had made. Yellow light from the streetlamps spilled across his sheets, and the night sounds began: a distant siren, a child's cry, a grunt in the dark. One by one he plucked off the fragile translucent wings, then he crushed the tiny purple body in his fist.

Chances of Survival

*C*ALVIN WAS AGAINST MOVING to Arizona from the start. In Idaho, he made his father stop the car, got out, and announced he was walking back to Montana. Dad let him go. He let Cal walk one maybe two miles, gave him time to think and get hungry, time to figure out that if he kept up a steady pace and didn't sleep, he could be home in two and a half days. Cal had the opportunity to review his resources: after rooting through all four pockets and fingering every fold, he came up with half a ticket to a movie, a key to a metal box he no longer had, a stick of gum that had gone through the washer, and twenty-seven cents. That might be enough for six candy bars if some lady behind the counter of a family grocery store in Sandpoint felt sorry for him and gave him two for seven. But even six candy bars wouldn't get him home. He knew he'd end up trying to steal a can of sardines or a package of hot dogs, and the fat lady would step in front of him as he tried to dart through the doorway. He saw the woman, just as if she was somebody he already knew. He saw her flabby arms quiver as she put her hands on her hips, and he saw the outline of her huge thighs through her dress as she stood with her back to the sun. No way she was going to take pity on a kid she didn't know who claimed he was walking to Montana.

By the time Calvin heard the car slow down behind him, he felt he didn't have a chance. Arms swinging, he kept pumping as if he meant to march all the way. His pants worked their way down his butt, and every twenty steps or so, he had to reach back and give them a yank. Cal wished his parents would make him get in the car. He imagined his mother sitting there saying, "Why won't that boy wear a belt?"

Finally, Dad pulled up beside him, and Mom rolled down her window. In the backseat, his two sisters pressed their faces to the window, flattening their lips and noses against the glass. Mom said, "Cal, it's almost two hundred miles to Bigfork, and once you get there you're going to find another family living in our house."

Cal squinted to keep from blinking and said, "I know that. Don't you think I know that?"

When he got back in the car, he made himself a cave on the floor by wedging a suitcase between the front and back seats. That's where he rode for three days, curled up and cramped in the dark.

Calvin's sister Dora wasn't happy either. The problem started with her hair. Mother said Arizona was hot and the kids would be in the pool all the time. She wasn't about to spend half the day untangling snarls. Two days before they left Montana, Mom took the girls to the beauty parlor and Dad took Cal to the barber.

Cal's hair was so short he could see his scalp. His ears stuck out too far and his neck was just plain skinny— there wasn't any other way to describe it. He didn't care; he didn't have to stare in the mirror. Allison's fine red hair looked very stylish, cut a little longer in front than it was in back so it curved in a pretty way around her jaw. But Dora's wasn't right. The pixie cut gave her cowlicks new determination. With sheets she'd torn into strips and colored with crayon, Dora made two braids and pinned them inside her baseball cap.

The apartment building in Scottsdale was low and flat, finished with the same sandy pink and gray speckled stone siding as every building as far as Cal could see. From the window of his attic bedroom in Montana, Cal had looked out at the jagged, violet peaks of the Mission Mountains and the stand of pines just beyond the yard. Here he gazed at a string of apartments along an endless strip of road, three-sided rectangular structures surrounded by hot cement. He imagined that in the courtyard of each one he would find a brilliant turquoise pool, glittering like a gaudy gem set in a dime-store ring.

Back home, Cal had often walked out onto the dock in the evening to stare across the dark, bottomless lake as the sun sank. He had ridden his bike along a logging road that took him deep into the hills. If some teenagers came rumbling along the road, he heard their jeep minutes before it appeared, and he had plenty of time to pull his bike into the bushes and crouch behind a rock. There was no need to see anyone. He had his own room and a lock with a key that worked.

He didn't want to ride his bike in Scottsdale. There wasn't a tree worth climbing; they were all dainty, flowering things with fragile limbs. The paved, dusty streets buzzed with cars: long, sleek Cadillacs and Buicks with the windows rolled up to keep the cool air inside. The only water was the tepid little pool, an unforgiving mirror of the blank sky.

Night was worse than day. Mom promised they wouldn't stay in the tiny apartment long, but two weeks passed and then a month; one by one, the boxes were unpacked. The apartment had only two bedrooms, so Calvin had to sleep with his sisters. Dad built him a wall of bookcases, but the barrier was only five feet high. When Cal had to be alone, he pulled a chair into his tight, airless closet and sat reading under the light of a bare bulb.

Each night, it took him longer and longer to fall asleep. He listened to Dora's heavy breath on the other side of the bookshelves. She rocked back and forth in her bed; springs creaked; a short, high moan was muffled by a pillow. Allison said, "Don't, baby; you're getting yourself all sweaty."

In the room on the other side of the wall, Cal's parents whispered. The thin walls seemed to disappear at night, to stand like flimsy shadows between the rooms. He knew his parents' tones. Sometimes their murmurs floated with the rhythm of a song, a sweet duet, but tonight Cal heard hushed hisses, arched words flung like stingers in the fuzzy darkness. "Shit," his father said, and the single sound was a stone falling. "How could you be?" He made no effort to speak softly.

"You know damn well how." Mother's voice was shrill, unguarded.

"Well, it's lousy timing."

"I didn't plan it."

"Obviously."

"And I didn't do it alone, either."

"I know that. But you should have . . ."

"I should have? I should have what?"

"Been more careful."

"It's hard to be careful when . . ."

"Say it."

"Let go of me."

"No. I want to hear you say it."

"You'll wake the children."

"Fine," Dad said, the word hard as a cuss. "Use the children. You always do."

Two doors slammed: first the bedroom, then the bathroom. Mom was too old to sit in her closet. Cal heard the water running in the tub for a long time. Finally Dad knocked on the door and said, "Come on, baby. I didn't mean it. Let's go to bed. Baby?" But Mom didn't answer and the water didn't stop.

Years ago, after a fight like this, Mom had packed a bag and said she was leaving. All three children lined up by the couch and begged her to stay. Dora was too small to understand, but Calvin and Allison thought they must have done something unforgivable to make Mommy want to run away. They couldn't figure out what it was, so they cried, choking out a dozen *sorry*'s until Mom was kneeling and crying and wiping their faces. Now Cal realized the bag she had was only big enough for a nightgown and two pairs of underwear, a toothbrush and a comb. They should have let her go, just so she'd know she could.

The water stopped at last, but Mom didn't come out of the bathroom. Cal had to pee. The more he thought about it, the worse it was. He had to go soon, or he wouldn't be able to walk.

He rapped on the door.

"Go away," Mom said. "Just let me have a few minutes to myself."

"Mom, it's Cal. I have to pee."

She opened the door, and Cal squinted at the glare of the fluorescent tube of light. The window was opened wide; the bathtub was full. Mom sat on the toilet, smoking, with her robe wrapped around her. The soapdish was full of white filters. Dad wouldn't let her smoke in front of the children. Many nights she sat by the bathroom window, watching the red pulse of the traffic light at the corner and smelling the cactus breeze that drifted off the desert after dark.

She stood up and lifted the lid of the toilet. "Go ahead," she said. "I won't watch."

"I can't go if you're listening."

Mom ruffled his hair and pulled the plug in the bathtub. "I'm too tired to sit up anyway," she said.

At first Allison wouldn't believe Cal when he told her Mom was pregnant. She said Mom was too old and that Dora was eight. A woman didn't get pregnant when her youngest child was already eight. Cal thought Allison was right. He couldn't think of any exceptions, but he knew what he'd heard, so he waited until his mother's belly began to swell and harden; he waited until she stopped wearing lipstick and her shoes didn't fit. Then Allison acted as if she'd known it all along. By June, Mom looked eight months pregnant instead of five. Her ankles grew thick and she slept most of the afternoon. Dora pretended not to notice. When people mentioned the baby, Dora tilted her head and stared at them the same way she stared at the worms on the sidewalk after a hard rain.

* * *

Dora and Calvin chased lizards at the playground behind the apartments. When Cal grabbed one by the tail, it fell off in his hand and the stubby lizard skittered away. Dora snatched one around the middle and stuffed it in a shoe box. Cal was twelve, four years older than Dora, but she was quicker. Cal put the blame on the fact that he was wearing his long bathrobe, and it slowed him down. He nabbed three tails and gave up. Dora asked him if the lizards would die without their tails, and he told her no, not to worry, that they'd grow new ones in a few days. She made him show her the tails. Already the heat had twisted and shriveled them. She said she didn't think the tails would grow new bodies, so Cal threw them in the shrubs and the children trotted home with the five lizards Dora had caught.

In a green lounge chair by the pool, Allison sat painting her toenails. She didn't want to see what her brother and sister had in the box. Even though Calvin was born ten months before Allison, everyone said she was more mature.

When each nail was pink and perfect, she pulled her sunglasses down over her eyes and leaned back in the chair. Her hands hung limply against the metal armrests. It's a poor family that can't afford one princess, Cal thought; that's what Mother always said.

Before noon, they usually had the pool to themselves. Later, the three Scofield boys took over, diving and splashing and raising such a ruckus that there wasn't room for anyone else. Cal didn't like them. For one thing, he couldn't keep them straight. They had interchangeable names: Mark, Luke, John. Their yellow hair was tinged green from the chlorine. Once he heard them ask Allison how a girl like her ended up with a brother who looked like the missing link. Allison didn't know what they meant, of course, but Calvin knew because the first day they met, the shortest Scofield boy had named him "Monkey Ears."

When the Scofields had worn themselves out, the ladies often appeared, their white clouds of hair floating around their dark faces. There were three of them too. Cal didn't know their names, so he called them each "Ma'am" and they liked that. To his face, they called him "young man," but when they whispered between themselves, they said "that sweet boy." If Calvin peered at the ladies from the window of the apartment, they looked like slim girls with very pale hair; but if he came out on the deck to talk to them, he could see a thousand fine wrinkles crisscrossing their brown skin. They put lotion on one another's back and legs. Cal watched them, thinking of crumpled paper bags smoothed flat with oil.

No one would come yet. Cal glanced at the sun: eleven o'clock. He padded up behind Allison's chair, and his shadow fell over her. Without raising her glasses she said, "Please don't block my sun, Cal. I'm timing this." She pointed to the black travel clock beside the chair. "Fifteen minutes from each angle. If you stand in my light, I won't be even."

Calvin didn't answer Allison, but he moved to the other end of the lounge chair and stood at her feet so his shadow dropped into the pool. Dora sat a hundred feet away in the shade, taking her lizards out of the box one by one and setting them free in the short grass. Cal's fingers moved in the pocket of his robe, pacing back and forth like tiny legs. The folds of the cloth were gritty with sand from the lizard tails. He wished he had caught one whole lizard so that he could let it go now.

In the hard, white light, Allison's pink toenails gleamed like sticky berries. Cal's fingers jumped in his pockets. He pinched sand between his fingers and flung both hands high in the air. The fine grains fell from his fingertips, sparkling like snowflakes in the sun and clinging to the bright polish. Allison bolted upright, jerking the sunglasses from her face. "You little shit," she said. She leaped for Cal, close to flying, and heaved them both in the water.

They struggled as they sank. Allison clawed at her brother's back, but the heavy bathrobe protected him. With his arms clamped around the girl's waist, Cal dragged her toward the bottom of the pool, thinking of himself as a great stone tied to her body. His cheeks were puffed fat with air; he believed he could last a long time. The robe floated up, billowing above his thighs, like the skirt of a dancer as she spins and twirls.

Allison stopped fighting. Cal thought they might both be dancers, that they would waltz down here to-gether where their bodies were so light and graceful. But

Allison's mouth gaped open, and her head jerked from side to side. Cal let her go, disappointed that she didn't try harder. He gave her a push toward the surface and watched her shoot away from him.

Dora leaned over the water, reaching out her hand to Allison, but studying Cal. He waved. She waved back—not a joyful, glad-to-see-you wave, but a tight, formal signal—then she dove. The jolt knocked her hat and cloth braids from her head, and they bobbed on the water as she swam down to her brother.

Bubbles poured from her mouth. Cal drew circles; she pointed toward the sky. The boy's chest was tight, as if the water made a wall in front of him and a wall behind and he was slowly being pressed between them. He nodded; yes, it was time to give up. He admitted to himself that he needed to breathe. Dora embraced Cal, and he went slack in her arms, glad to let something happen to him; to be rescued. He felt the force of Dora's kicks, felt her fight against her lack of breath and his dead weight. Above him, the water looked hard, a wavy sheet of clear metal they would have to break. The blaze of light blinded him. When he closed his eyes, he saw a scatter of red squares on black. Then he was gasping, gulping down air. The water wasn't shattered: it closed around their shoulders, a comforting thing.

Underneath Allison's lounge chair, the alarm clock jangled, reminding her it was time to turn over. The children were all out of the pool, but no one moved to quiet the frantic black box.

"Shut that damn thing off!" Mother yelled from the doorway. She waddled toward her children; her bare feet slapped the pavement, and her back arched with the strain of her belly.

"What are you doing?" she said to Dora. "I told you not to wear your clothes in the pool. And I told you why. The chlorine takes all the color out. You've ruined those shorts." The blue dye was bleeding from the cloth and running in rivulets down Dora's thighs. "Where is that clock?" Dora pointed to the chair, her face blank as an egg. "Well, turn it off, will you?"

With thick, slow steps, Dora moved like a person who was still submerged. "Today, Dora," Mom said, "today."

When the buzzing stopped, Mother turned to Calvin. "And what are you up to? Are you going to wear that robe in the pool too? Well, you'll drown if you do and you'll have no one to blame but yourself."

Mother peered at first one child and then the next. "No one is going swimming today. Do you hear me?" She was yelling; everyone in the whole apartment building probably heard her. "I don't care if it gets up to a hundred degrees. I don't care if it gets up to a hundred and twenty."

"Well, Calvin," she said, "you may as well give me that robe to wash. It's soaking wet. You can't wear it anyway." She'd been trying to get the robe from him for six weeks: "Just for an hour, Cal; it's filthy," she'd say. Finally she made a deal with him instead—he had to produce one pair of undershorts a day, and she washed them faithfully, even after Allison informed her that Cal cheated and gave her clean ones sometimes.

Just the night before, Cal's father had had one of those talks with him about the robe. "I'm sure you have your reasons, Cal, but you're driving your mother crazy. It's such a small thing; can't you give up the robe?" But it wasn't a small thing at all—wearing the robe was part of the most important thing in the world, and it was all tangled up now, so he couldn't explain it. He told his father that Mother didn't care. Cal thought of her by the sink, the dirty soapsuds dropping from her hands onto the floor as she said it: "I don't care, Cal. Do what you want. Do whatever you damn well please."

Cal plopped down on the lounge chair. "I don't need to take it off," he said. "It will dry out." In the middle of the pool, Dora's hat and braids sank slowly.

The children couldn't have gone swimming anyway. By afternoon, a stiff breeze whipped itself into fierce gusts, churning the sand to dust demons. The desert wind drove the heat deeper into the lungs and under the skin. When the squall died down, a gray scum had settled on the pool.

All day, Calvin's robe stayed damp, but he didn't take it off. He wondered what would happen to him if he stopped wearing it now. The robe wasn't the beginning, or even the main thing—using it just happened along the way, and now it seemed necessary, irreversible.

Cal thought the whole idea started when he was still in Montana. Dad said they had to go to church one last time; that was the right thing to do even though they hadn't gone for three months, not since Christmas. The girls complained. Mother said she had too much to do to get all dressed up. But Cal didn't mind. He liked church; he thought of it as a contest: *How straight can I sit? Can I hear my own voice when everyone around me is singing louder? How long can I hold my breath?* Usually Reverend Sykes's sermon was a drone that filled Cal's chest, the hum of a thousand bees, wordless and wise. This day was different. Cal listened to the words so hard that his toes curled tight inside his stiff shoes.

Reverend Sykes said, God thinks about man all the time, and that is why we have life and breath on this good earth. But man hardly thinks about God at all. Every time a man stops thinking about God, that man is in danger, and God is in danger.

It was just a small part of the sermon. At first Cal was surprised people didn't stand up and make the reverend stop to explain exactly what he meant. But like most things in church, a lot of folks missed it. Dad's head drooped and a flutter of air escaped between his lips. Allison sat with her white-gloved hands folded in her lap, a perfect little lady, but she wasn't thinking about what the man had just said; she was thinking about herself, about what a good girl she was to sit there so still, her lips a soft, unsmiling, angelic curve. Dora swung her feet back and forth. She had learned the whole alphabet in sign language and was talking to herself with her hands. Only Mother heard what he said, and she saw that Cal heard too and that he thought it was a remarkable thing. She put her hand over his and looked at him as if to say: *Yes, Cal, that's all of it, thinking about God.*

All the way to Arizona, Cal tried to figure it out. He was afraid to ask anyone. The way Reverend Sykes had said it, so casually, on his way to saying something else, Cal thought maybe everyone except him knew all about it. Sometimes, after dinner, he noticed his father gazing at a bare spot on the wall, and he would ask Dad what he was thinking. But the answer was never what he hoped: Dad was always thinking about the wiring of the bank he was designing or whether or not he'd remembered to mail the insurance check. Cal got the same kinds of answers from Mom: Do you want tuna casserole for dinner tonight, or would you like cheese dreams? He had the idea that hardly anyone knew how critical it was to think about God.

If God stopped thinking about him, Cal knew what would happen. He would vanish, not just disappear, but cease to exist. He would have no past, and no one would remember him—not even Mom and Dad. But he didn't have to worry about that because God's mind was bigger than the whole world. God kept all of the people in his thoughts at once, and it wasn't a struggle: it was a comfort, and he was glad to do it.

A man's mind was pitiful compared with God's. A person had to concentrate just to keep a few ideas in his head. He was so busy worrying about what to put in his stomach or what he and his wife might do later that night when the kids were in bed that he didn't have room in his brain for anything else.

Cal wondered what would happen if a whole lot of men forgot to think about God for a long time. God took care of the people, but who kept God alive? Since men's minds were so small and so easily cluttered, it must take thousands of people to keep God from vanishing.

Cal tried to do his share, but he had a hard time: he thought about himself too much. While he lay awake at night, Cal tried to concentrate on God, but the whispers beyond the wall and the moans of his sister on the other side of the bookcase made his mind wander. He knew that prayers should be offerings and not requests; still, he found himself asking God to let him sleep. Dark circles formed under his eyes and made him look like an old man. One day, he decided he wasn't well enough to get dressed; he was weak and his head was fuzzy, so he wore the heavy maroon bathrobe all day. He wore it the next day and the next. A strange thing had happened, he realized that if he wore the robe, he thought less about himself, as if the parts of his body that were covered couldn't distract him anymore and only the useful parts were left: his feet for walking, his hands for helping, his head for thinking about the one important thing.

He wasn't perfect. Sometimes he used his toes for picking up pennies off the floor; his hands strayed: he shuffled cards. He thought about the white-haired ladies and wondered if their sheets were soaked with the oil they put all over their bodies. He thought about his father swearing in the dark and his mother's baby. He imagined what Dora was doing when she made the bed squeak night after night. He was getting better, though, and the robe helped. Just the weight of it and the scratchy cloth on his neck reminded him to clear his mind.

The cement was so hot it burned the bottoms of Cal's feet unless he ran. He saw it all, right after the sandstorm, saw the three Scofield boys knock a bird nest out of the tree on purpose, so the chicks would fall on the sidewalk and their stomachs would burn. The baby finches weren't dead yet, but Cal couldn't pick them up because their unfeathered flesh stuck to the blistering pavement. The mother flew in circles, railing, giving Cal steady abuse as he crouched beside her floundering offspring.

Cal's mother followed him. "It's no use to watch; come inside," she said. When the boy didn't move, she put her hand on his head and he twisted away. He didn't let her touch him anymore; this was one of his rules, and he had to be especially careful because sometimes, when he was hot or tired, nothing felt better to him than her dry cool fingers on his forehead or cheeks.

She shuffled inside, but in a few minutes she returned to try again. Cal had found something. He knelt in the shade with his hands cupped. As Mother came closer, he held his hands up to her, an offering, a puny-winged, bald fledgling with its eyes glued shut.

"This one's alive," he said. The chick was so light in his hands, so round and pink, nearly featherless; she wasn't like a bird at all, more like a small peeping heart. "She was in the grass," Cal whispered.

Mother looked at the other baby finches; they were dead now. "It doesn't have a chance, Cal," she said. "It's too young; it needs its mother."

"Then we'll fix the nest and put it back in the tree," Cal said.

"The mother won't take care of it now, not after a person has touched it."

"I had to," Cal said. "How else could I . . ."

"I'm not blaming you," Mother said. "She couldn't have gotten it back to the nest by herself anyway."

"Then we have to try. It won't hurt just to try."

She couldn't make him leave it in the grass, not while its wings still fluttered and its feet twitched, so they made a bed of grass for it in Dora's discarded shoe box.

Dad didn't say a word when he looked over Cal's shoulder to see what he had in the box. Mom was in the kitchen, cutting vegetables; Cal could see her from where he sat in the living room. Allison skipped down the hall, leaping at Dad to be crushed in one of his bear hugs.

"How's my girl?" he said. He looked behind her. "Where's your sister?"

Allison cocked her head. "She's in the bedroom. She lost her braids in the pool, and she hasn't come out all day."

Dad snorted and sauntered into the kitchen. He put one hand on Mother's hip and reached for a carrot with his other hand. "Rough day?" he said, massaging the lowest part of her back. She nodded. He muttered, "What the hell is he doing with that bird?"

"Shush, Stan, he'll hear you."

Dad stopped rubbing and leaned against the counter. "I mean for him to hear me. What were you thinking, letting him bring it in the house? Birds carry all sorts of diseases."

Calvin was only twelve feet away. His parents had gotten into the habit of talking about him that way, as if he were deaf or senile. One night not long ago, Cal was standing at the window and they were sitting on the couch behind him. Mother said, "I'm at the end of my rope. I don't know what to do with him these days. If he doesn't straighten up by August, I think we should consider a special school." Dad asked her what she had in mind. "Well, I was wondering," she said, "about a military school. He'd have some rules, you know, and learn some discipline." Calvin stared at the window, but not outside; he studied his own reflection: the narrow, pale face, the ears and hands that were too big for the boy who stood there with his shoulders hunched beneath a dark robe.

In the kitchen, Dad wouldn't let up about the damn bird. He made it sound like it was all Mother's fault and she'd done a stupid thing, letting Cal bring it inside. But his voice wasn't rough anymore, and he inched closer to her, so close that she must have felt his breath on her neck as she chopped the last stalk of celery. He was reaching for her again, his hands were almost on her shoulders. Cal tried not to watch.

Mother whirled, slicing the air under Dad's nose with the paring knife she held clutched in her hand. "What would you have done?" she said. "It's the first thing he's cared about since we got here."

"And what's he going to care about tomorrow when he finds the putrid thing stiff in its box?" Dad had jumped away from her and was halfway across the room, shouting now.

Allison stood in the shadows of the hallway, waiting, and Dora opened her door an inch to listen. The children knew that if Mom and Dad kept at it, there wouldn't be any dinner. Dad would have to pile them all in the car and take them out for burgers; Mom would go to her room for the rest of the night and wouldn't answer no matter who knocked. Calvin froze. This was a trick he'd discovered. If he stayed perfectly still, time didn't pass and nothing happened. Mother said, "I don't know what he'll care about if that pathetic bird dies. I'm hoping for this one small miracle." Her voice was weary, defeated, a thin white flag waving in the dull heat.

Cal breathed again and called to Allison. "Look," he said. Allison glanced in the box. "She's better, don't you think? Watch." He showed her how the chick tilted her head back and took water from an eyedropper. "See, she's going to be okay." Allison shifted her weight to one leg and leaned against her brother. Already the morning seemed like a long time ago, like a dream that made him stop breathing: he'd awakened gasping for air, wondering if he might have died if he had stayed asleep a minute longer. He'd had burning dreams and falling dreams: the house in Montana was on fire, and he had to jump from his attic window. But the dreams where he drowned were the worst; he was trapped beneath a dock, and no one could see him.

The baby finch opened its gaping mouth. "She's a survivor," Cal said. "I know it."

"Sure she is," Allison said. She looked at its wrinkled skin and useless wings, and Cal knew she was thinking about what Dad had said, that Cal would find the bird stiff in its box.

"Mom said she didn't have a chance, but look at her. She wants to be alive," he said. "That's why she landed in the grass instead of on the cement. I bet she flew. Can't you just see her, flapping like crazy to get to the grass?"

He knew this wasn't true. He saw the boys with the stick, the broken nest toppling out of the tree, all the warm fledglings tumbling head over tail. One lucky one landed in the shade, out of sight, so none of the boys noticed it or flung it onto the cement. Cal was afraid now, afraid to think that the chick's survival had nothing to do with flying or how much he wanted her to stay alive. He tried to understand how all that could be a matter of chance, nothing more than a safe fall and an unexpected rescue.

Mother called Allison to come set the table. Cal's sister squeezed his hand, and he didn't pull away even though it felt good. His heart beat as fast as the heart of the chick had beat against his hands. He was scared when she touched him and scared when she let go. Dora appeared in the hallway with a towel wrapped around her head, and Cal had to keep himself from laughing. But he didn't laugh because Dora had pulled him from the pool when he was too tired or too stubborn to save himself. "Come here," he said. "I want to show you something." Carefully, Dora stepped out of the shadows. The light in the living room made her stiffen, ready to flee, so Cal kept talking, reeling her in an inch at a time until she stood beside him. The finch peeped, her voice surprisingly strong.

When they sat down to dinner, Mother was still and calm, her fingers laced across her full lap. The fan in the kitchen beat at the dead air. Dad bowed his head and said, "Father we thank thee for these mercies." Mom said she was too hot to eat, so Dad dampened a cloth and washed her forehead and her wrists. He told her to put her feet on his lap, and he washed each toe separately right there at the table; then he told her a story about a storekeeper in Phoenix who was so afraid of pregnant women he wouldn't let them shop in his place. "What does he think," Mom said, "that they'll have their babies right there?" She laughed, thinking about the bald little man backed into a corner with his eyes closed. "Or does he think they'll sit on him?" This made her laugh harder, deep, full chuckles, loud as a man's; her huge stomach shook, and the cloth of her dress stretched so tight Cal thought she would burst out of it. Dad washed her dimpled knees and said, "I'll take you down there someday; you can give him a good scare."

"Then I better fatten myself up," Mom said, patting her bulge as if it belonged to someone else. She ate two pork chops and a mound of mashed potatoes. Dad got up again and again to run water through the cloth.

One by one, the children asked to be excused, but Cal's parents sat at the table for a long time, until the kitchen was dark, until the air drifting through the screen door was cool.

The street was quiet now, and Cal heard voices wafting across the courtyard; they were the soft voices of evening, and he imagined all the families just like his own, the arguments that had dissolved in the dizzy heat of a fading afternoon; these were the voices of people who had been pulled from the water at the last moment, the songs of the children who jumped out of the flames with their eyes screwed shut and somehow, by some small miracle, still landed in the net.

Iona Moon

$\mathcal{W}$ILLY HAMILTON NEVER DID like Iona Moon. He said country girls always had shit on their shoes and he could smell her after she'd been in his car. Jay Tyler said his choice of women was nobody's business, and if Willy didn't like it, he should keep his back doors locked.

Choice of women, Jay said that so nice. He thought Iona was a woman because the first night they were together he put his hand under her shirt and she didn't stop kissing him. He inched his fingers under her brassiere, like some five-legged animal, until his wrist was caught by the elastic and his hand was squished against her breast. She said, "Here, baby, let me help you," and she reached around behind her back and released the hooks. One hand on each breast, Jay Tyler whistled through his

107

teeth. "Sweet Jesus," he said, and unbuttoned her blouse, his fingers clumsy and stiff with the fear that she might change her mind. Jay Tyler had known plenty of girls, girls who let him do whatever he wanted as long as he could take what he was after without any assistance on their part, without ever saying, "Yes, Jay," the way Iona did, just a murmur, "yes," soft as snow on water.

In the moonlight, her skin was pale, her breasts small but warm, something a boy couldn't resist. Jay cupped them in his palms, touching the nipples with the very tips of his fingers, as if they were precious and alive, something separate from the girl, something that could still be frightened and disappear. He pressed his lips to the hard bones of Iona Moon's chest, rested his head in the hollow between her breasts and whispered words no boy had ever spoken to her.

He said, "Thank you, oh God, thank you." His voice was hushed and amazed, the voice of a drowning man just pulled from the river. As his mouth found her nipple, Jay Tyler closed his eyes tight, as if he wanted to be blind, and Iona Moon almost laughed to see his sweet face wrinkle that way; she couldn't help thinking of the newborn pigs, their little eyes glued shut, scrambling for a place at their mother's teats.

Iona supposed Willy Hamilton was right about her shoes, but she was past noticing it herself. Every morning, she got up early to milk the four cows. Mama had always done it before Iona and her brothers were awake. Even in the winter, Hannah Moon trudged to the barn while it was still dark, slogged through the mud and slush, wearing her rubber boots and Daddy's fur-lined coat that she could have wrapped around herself twice. The waves of blue snow across the fields fluttered, each drift a breast heaving, giving up its last breath.

Mama said she liked starting the day that way, in the lightless peace God made before he made the day, sitting with your cheek pressed against the cow's warm flank, your hands on her udder, understanding your pull has to be strong and steady but not too hard, knowing she likes you there and she feels grateful in the way cows do, so she makes a sleepy sound like a moan or a hum, the same sound Iona heard herself make at the edge of a dream.

Willy had a girl, Belinda Beller. She wore braces, and after gym class, Iona saw her stuff her bra with toilet paper. Willy and Belinda, Iona and Jay, parked down by the river in Willy's Chevy. Belinda kept saying, "No, honey, please, I don't want to." Jay panted over Iona, licking her neck, slipping his tongue as far in her ear as it would go; her bare back stuck to the vinyl seat, and Willy said, "I'm sorry." His voice was serious and small. "I'm sorry." He said it again, like a six-year-old who had killed his own gerbil by mistake.

Willy thought of his father handcuffing that boy who stole the floodlights from the funeral home. Willy was twelve and liked cruising with his dad, pretending they might get lucky and find some trouble. They caught up with the boy down by the old Miller Creek bridge. His white face rose like a moon above his dark clothes, his eyes enchanted to stone by the twin beams of the headlights.

Horton Hamilton climbed out of the patrol car, one hand on his hip. The thick fingers unsnapped the leather band that held the pistol safe in the holster. Willy's father said, "Don't you be gettin' any ideas of makin' like a jackrabbit, boy; I got a gun." He padded toward the skittery, long-legged kid, talking all the time, using the low rumble of his voice to hold the boy in one place, like a farmer trying to mesmerize a dog that's gone mad, so he can put a bullet through its head.

Willy recognized the kid. His name was Matt Fry and he lived out west of town on the Kila Flats, a country boy. Horton Hamilton believed you could scare the mischief out of a child. He cuffed Matt Fry as if he were a grown man who'd done a lot worse. He said stealing those lights was no petty crime: they were worth a lot of money, enough to make the theft a felony even though Matt Fry was only fifteen years old.

A policeman didn't get much action in White Falls, Idaho, so Horton Hamilton took what business he had seriously. He'd drawn his gun any number of times, or put his hand on it at least, but he'd had cause to shoot only once in nineteen years, and that was to kill a badger that had taken up residence on poor Mrs. Griswold's porch and refused to be driven away by more peaceable means.

Fear of God, fear of the devil, that was good for a boy, but Willy heard later that Matt Fry's parents had had enough of his shenanigans and that a felony was the limit, the very limit. They told the county judge they'd lost control of their boy and it would be best for everyone to lock him up and set him straight. Until then, Willy didn't know that if you did a bad enough thing, your parents could decide they didn't want you anymore.

When Matt Fry came back from the boys' home, he smelled like he forgot sometimes and pissed his own pants; he didn't look at you if you saw him on the street and said, "Hey." His parents still wouldn't let him come home and he slept in a burned-out barn down in the gully. People said Matt Fry got caught fighting his first day at the state home. They threw him in the hole for eighteen days, all by himself, without any light, and when they dragged him out he was like this: lame in one foot, mumbling syllables that didn't add up to words, skinny as a coyote at the end of winter.

Willy stopped pawing at Belinda and sat with his hands in his lap until she leaned over to peck his cheek and say, "It's all right now, honey." Iona Moon had no sympathy for Belinda Beller's point of view. What sense was there in saving everything up for some special occasion that might not ever come? How do you hold a boy back if it feels good when he slides his knee between your legs? How do you say *no* when his tongue in your ear makes you arch your back and grab his hair?

Willy liked nice girls, girls who accidentally brushed
their hands against a guy's crotch, girls who wiggled
their butts when they walked past you in the hall, threw
their shoulders back and almost closed their eyes when
they said hello. Girls who could pull you right up to the
edge and still always, always say no.

Iona thought, you hang on to something too long,
you start to think it's worth more than it is. She was
never that way on account of having three brothers and
being the youngest. When she was nine, her oldest
brother gave her a penny to dance for him. Before long,
they made it regular. Night after night Iona twirled
around the barn for Leon, spun in the circle of light from
the lantern hanging off the rafter. Dale and Rafe started
coming too; she earned three cents a night from her
brothers and saved every penny till she had more than
four dollars. Later they gave her nickels for lifting her
shirt and letting them touch the buds that weren't breasts
yet. And one time, when Leon and Iona were alone in
the loft, he paid her a dime for lying down and letting
him rub against her. She was scared, all that grunting
and groaning, and when she looked down she saw that
his little prick wasn't little anymore: it was swollen and
dark and she yelled, "You're hurting yourself." He
clamped his dirty hand over her mouth and hissed. Finally he made a terrible sound, like the wail a cow makes
when her calf is halfway out of her; his mouth twisted
and his face turned red, as if Iona had choked him. But
she hadn't; her arms were flung straight out from her

sides; her hands clutched fistfuls of straw. Leon collapsed on his sister like a dead man, and she lay there wondering how she was going to explain to Mama and Daddy that she'd killed him. He crushed the breath out of her; sweat from his face trickled onto hers, and she felt something damp and sticky soaking through her jeans. When she tried to wriggle out from under him, he sprang back to life. He pinched her face with one hand. Squeezing her cheeks with his big fingers, he said, "Don't you ever tell, Iona. Mama will hate you if you ever tell."

After that her brothers stopped paying her to dance for them, and Leon made Rafe and Dale cut their thumbs with his hunting knife and swear by their own blood that they'd never tell anyone what they did in the barn that year.

You can't make my brothers do much of anything unless you force them to swear in blood, Iona thought.

One morning after a storm, she tramped out to the barn to do her milking. The wind howled, cutting through her jeans. Snow had drifted against the door; she bent over and dug like a dog. The first stall was empty. She ran to the next, shining her flashlight in every corner, trying to believe a cow could hide in a shadow like a cat, but she knew, even as she ran in circles, she knew that all four cows were out in the fields, that her brothers had just assumed an animal will head for shelter on its own. They didn't know cows the way Iona and her mama did. A cow's hardly any smarter than a chicken; a cow has half the brains of a pig; a cow's like an overgrown child, like the Wilkerson boy, who grew tall and fat but never got smart.

She heard them. As she ran across the fields, stumbling in the snow, falling on her face more than once and snorting ice through her nose, she heard them crying like old women. The four of them huddled together, standing up past their knees in the drifts. Snow had piled in ridges down their backs; they hadn't moved all night. They let out that sound, that awful wail, as if their souls were being torn out of them. Iona had to whip them with her belt to get them going; that's how cows are: they'll drop to their knees and freeze to death with their eyes wide open and the barn door barely a hundred feet in front of them.

Later, Iona took Mama her aspirin and hot milk, sat on the edge of her bed and moaned like the cows, closing her eyes and stretching her mouth wide as it would go. Mama breathed deep with laughter, holding her stomach; the milk sloshed in the cup and Iona had to hold it. Mama had a bad time holding on to things. Her fingers were stiff and twisted, and that winter, her knees swelled up so big she couldn't walk.

Iona Moon told Jay Tyler how it was in the winter on the Kila Flats, how the wind had nothing to stand in its way, how the water froze in the pipes and you had to use the outhouse, how you held it just as long as you could because the snow didn't fall, it blew straight in your face;

splinters of ice pierced your skin and you could go blind or lose your way just walking to that little hut twenty-five yards behind the house. She told him she kept a thunder mug under her bed in case she had to pee in the night. But she didn't tell him her mama had to use a bedpan all the time, and Iona was the one who slid it under her bony butt because Mama said it wasn't right for the man you love to see you that way.

Mama knew Iona had a guy. She made Iona tell her that Jay Tyler was on the diving team in the summer. He could fly off the high board backward, do two somersaults and half a twist; he seemed to open the water with his hands, and his body made a sound like a flat stone you spin sideways so it cuts without a splash: blurp, that's all. Mama worked the rest of it out of Iona too. Jay's father was a dentist with a pointed gray beard and no hair. Jay was going to college so he could come back to White Falls and go into business with his dad. Iona said it as if she was proud, but Mama shook her head and blinked hard at her gnarled hands, trying to make something go away. She said, "If I was a strong woman, Iona, I'd lock you in this house till you got over that boy. I'd rather have you hate me than see your heart be broke."

"Jay's not like that," Iona said.

"Every boy's like that in the end. Dentists don't marry the daughters of potato farmers. He'll be lookin' for a girl with an education." She didn't talk that way to be mean. Iona knew Mama loved her more than anyone alive.

* * *

Willy thought that just listening to Jay Tyler and his father might be dangerous, a bad thing that made his stomach thump like a second heart. Horton Hamilton had raised his son to believe there was one way that was right and one way that was wrong and nothing, absolutely nothing, in between. Willy said, "What if someone steals food because he's hungry?" And his father said, "Stealing's wrong." Willy said, "If a man's dying, if he feels his whole body filling up with pain, would the Lord blame him for taking his own life?" Horton Hamilton rubbed his chin. "The Lord would *forgive* him, Willy, because that's the good Lord's way, but no man has the right to choose his time of death, or any other man's time of death." Willy thought he had him now: "Why do you carry a gun?" His father said his gun was to warn and to wound, but only if there was no other way. He liked talking better.

Willy remembered the way his father talked to Matt Fry. He saw Matt Fry hobbling down the middle of the street, his head bobbing, his pants crusted with dirt, smelling of piss. He thought maybe Matt Fry would have been better off if his father had shot him dead at Miller Creek. And he bowed his head with the shame of letting himself think it.

Jay Tyler's dad wanted to be a lawyer but became a dentist like his own father instead. He taught Jay to argue both sides of every question with equal passion. When Willy told him there was one right and one wrong and all you had to do was look in the Bible to see which was which, Andrew Johnson Tyler scratched his bald head and said, "Well, Willy, I tell you, it's hard for a *medical man* to believe in God." Willy couldn't figure out why, but there was something about the way Dr. Tyler said "medical man," some secret reverence, that made Willy afraid to question him.

Jay's mother floated across the veranda, her footsteps so soft that Willy glanced at her feet to be sure they touched wood. The folds of her speckled dress fell forward and back; Willy saw the outline of her thighs and had to look away. "All this talk, all this talk," she said. "How about some lemonade? I'm so dry I could choke." Everything about her was pale: her cheeks, flushed from the heat; the sweep of yellow hair, wound in a bun but not too tight; a few blond tendrils swirling at the nape of her neck, damp with her own sweat; the white dress with tiny pink roses, cut low in front so that when she leaned forward and said, "Why don't you help me, Willy," he saw the curve of her breasts.

In the kitchen she brushed his hair from his eyes, touched his hand, almost as if she didn't mean to do it, but he knew. He scurried out to the porch with the lemonade on a tray, ice rattling against glass. From the cool shadows of the house, he swore he heard a woman holding her laughter in her throat.

Willy lost his way on the Kila Flats. All those dirt roads looked the same. Jay told him: "Turn left, turn right, take another right at the fork"; he sent Willy halfway around the county so he'd have time in the backseat with Iona Moon, time to unhook her bra, time to unzip his pants. Willy kept looking in the rearview mirror; he'd dropped Belinda Beller off hours ago. He imagined his father cruising Main and Woodvale Park, looking for him. He imagined his mother at the window, parting the drapes with one hand, pressing her nose to the glass. She worried. She saw a metal bumper twisted around a tree, a wheel spinning a foot above the ground, headlights blasting into the black woods. She washed the blood off the faces of the four teenagers, combed their hair, dabbed their bruises with flesh-colored powder, painted their blue lips a fresh, bright pink. That was back in '57, but she saw their open eyes and surprised mouths every time Willy was late. "Forgive me, Lord, for not trusting you. I know my thoughts are a curse. I know he's safe with you, Lord, and he's a good boy, a careful boy, but I can't help my worrying, Lord: he's my only son. I love my girls, but he's special, you see, in that way." She unlaced her fingers and hissed, "I'll thrash his hide when he walks in that door." She said it out loud because God only listened to prayers and silence. He was too busy to pay attention to all the clatter of words spoken in ordinary tones.

Jay said, "Shit, Willy, you took the wrong turn back there. I told you *right* at the fork." And Willy said he did go right, and Jay answered, "We'd be in front of Iona's house if you went right." There was something in Jay's

voice, a creak or a gurgle in the throat, that gave him
away. Willy slammed the brakes; his Chevy did a quarter
spin that threw Jay and Iona against the door. "What the
hell?" said Jay.

"Get out," Willy said.

"What?"

"You heard me. Get out of my car."

Jay zipped his pants and opened the door; Iona
started to climb out after him. "Just Jay," Willy said, and
he got out too. The front window was cracked open
enough for Iona to hear Willy say, "You're gonna get me
grounded because you wanna fool around with that little
slut." Jay shoved Willy over the hood of the car, and Iona
watched the dust curl in the streams of yellow light,
waiting for the blow. But Jay didn't hit him; he held him
there, leaning on top of him, ten seconds, twenty; and
when he let Willy up, Jay clapped him on the shoulder,
said, "Sorry, buddy, I'll make it up to you."

Jay stood on the diving board, lean and tan, unbeatable.
Willy was almost as good, some days better; but next to
Jay he was pale and scrawny, unconvincing. Jay rolled
off the balls of his feet, muscles flexing from his calves to
his thighs. He threw an easy one first, a single somersault
in lay-out position. As he opened up above the water,
Iona gasped, expecting him to swoop back into the air.

Willy did the same dive, nearly as well. All day they
went on this way, first one, then the other; Jay led Willy
by a point and a half; the rest of the field dropped by ten.

Jay saved the backward double somersault with a twist for last. He climbed the ladder slowly, as if he had to think about the dive rung by rung. His buttocks bunched up tight, clenched like fists. On the board, he rolled his shoulders, shook his hands, his feet. He strutted to the end, raised his arms, and spun on his toes. Every muscle frozen, he grit his teeth and leaped, clamped his knees to his chest and heaved head over heel, once, twice, opened up and twisted, his limbs straight as a drill.

But in that last moment, Jay Tyler's concentration snapped. By some fluke, some sudden weakness, his knees bent and his feet slapped the water.

Iona thought she'd see Jay spit with disgust as he gripped the gutter of the pool, but he came up grinning, flashing his straight, white teeth, his father's best work. Willy offered his hand. "I threw it too hard, buddy," Jay said. Buddy. Iona stood outside the chain-link fence; she barely heard it, but it made her think of that dusty road; stars flung in the cool black sky by a careless hand; Willy pinned to the hood of the car; and Jay saying: *Sorry, buddy, I'll make it up to you.* Only this way, Willy would never know. It was just like Jay not to give a damn about blame or forgiveness.

Willy's dive was easier, two somersaults without a twist, but flawless. He crept ahead of Jay and no one else touched their scores. They sauntered to the bathhouse with their arms around each other's shoulders, knowing they'd won the day.

Standing in the dappled light beneath an oak, Jay Tyler's mother hugged Willy and Jay, and his father pumped their hands. Willy wished his parents could have seen him, this day above all others, but his father was on duty; and old lady Griswold had died, so his mother was busy making her look prettier than she ever was.

Iona Moon shuffled toward them, head down, eyes on the ground. Willy nudged Jay. In a single motion, graceful as the dive he almost hit, Jay turned, smiled, winked, and flicked his wrist near his thigh, a wave that said everything: go away, Iona; can't you see I'm with *my parents?* Willy felt the empty pit of his stomach, a throb of blood in his temples that made him dizzy, as if he were the one shooed away, as if he slunk in the shadows and disappeared behind the thick trunk of the tired tree, its limbs drooping with their own weight.

He was ashamed, like the small boy squinting under the fluorescent lights of the bathroom. His mother stripped his flannel pajamas off him with quick, hard strokes and said, "You're *soaked*, Willy; you're absolutely *drowned*."

Upstairs the air was still and hot, but Hannah Moon couldn't stand the noise of the fan and told Iona, no, please, don't turn it on. Iona said, "I'm going to town tonight, Mama. You want anything?"

"Why don't you just stay here and read to me till I fall asleep? What are you planning in town?"

"Nothing, nothing at all in particular. I get this desire, you know. It's so dark out here at night, just our little lights and the black fields and the blacker hills. I want to see a whole blaze of lights, all the streetlamps going on at once, all the houses burning—like something's about to happen. You have to believe something's going to happen."

"Don't you go looking for him," Mama said. "Don't you go looking for that boy. I know he hasn't called you once since school got out. Bad enough what he did, but don't you go making it worse by being a fool."

"He's nothing to me, Mama. You want a treat or something, maybe a magazine?"

"Take a dollar from my jewelry box and get me as much chocolate as that'll buy. And don't you tell your daddy, promise?"

"Promise."

"He thinks it's not good for me; I think I've got to have some pleasure."

Daddy sat on the porch with Leon and Rafe and Dale. They rocked in the great silence of men, each with his pipe, each with the same tilt of the head as if a single thought wove through their minds. A breeze high in the pines made the tops sway so the limbs rubbed up against one another. The sound they made was less than a breath, a whisper in a dream or the last thing your mother said before she kissed you good night. You were too small to understand the words, but you knew from her voice that you were loved and safe; the kiss on your forehead was a whisper too, a promise no one could keep.

Iona buzzed up and down Main, feeling strong riding up high in the cab of Daddy's red truck, looking down on cars and rumbling over potholes too fast. Daddy kept a coil of rope, a hacksaw and a rifle in the back behind the seat. She had no intention, no intention at all, but she swung down Willow Glen Road, past Jay Tyler's house. She honked her horn at imaginary children in the street, stomped on her brakes and laid rubber to avoid a cat that wasn't there; but all that noise didn't lure anyone out of the Tyler house, and no lights popped on upstairs or down. In the green light of dusk, the house looked gray and cool, a huge lifeless thing waiting to crumble.

She sped toward Seventh, Willy Hamilton's street. She might just happen to roll by, and maybe in the course of conversation she'd say, "Are the Tylers out of town?" Not that she cared; she was only mildly curious. "The house looks absolutely deserted," she'd say. "I don't know why anyone would want to live in that big old thing."

Sure enough, Willy stood in the driveway, hosing down his sky-blue Chevrolet. Iona leaned out the window. "Hey, Willy," she said. He wrinkled up his forehead and didn't say anything. Iona was undaunted. "You wanna go get an ice cream with me?" she said. The spray from the hose made a clear arc before it spattered on the cement and trickled toward the gutter in thick muddy rivulets.

Willy was feeling sorry for her in a way. But he still didn't like her, and he didn't think he could stand the smell of her truck. He told himself to be brave; it wouldn't last long, and it was such a small thing to do, such a small, kind gesture; then he felt very proud, overcome with the realization that he was going to do this good thing.

He was still thinking how generous he was when they finished their cones and Iona jolted out along the river road instead of heading toward his house. He said, "Where are you going?" And she said, "The river." He told her he needed to get home; it was almost dark. Iona said, "I know." He told her he meant it, but his voice was feeble, and she kept plowing through the haze of dusk, faster and faster, till the whole seat was shaking.

She swerved down to the bank of the river, where all the kids came to park; but it was too early for that, so they were alone. Willy stared at the water, at the beer bottles bobbing near the shore, and the torn-off limb of a tree being dragged downstream. "I'm sorry about Jay," he said.

"Why're you sorry? He's not dead."

"He didn't treat you right."

Iona slid across the seat so her thigh pressed against Willy's thigh. "Would you treat me right?" she said. He tried to inch away, but there was nowhere to go. Iona's hand rested on his knee, then started moving up his leg, real slow. Willy swatted it away. "You still think I'm a slut?" Iona said. She touched his thigh again, lightly, higher than before. "I'm not a slut, Willy; I'm just more *generous* than most girls you know." She clutched his wrist and tried to pull his closed hand to her breast. "Don't be afraid," she said. "You won't be fingering Kleenex when you get a grip on my titties." Willy looked so confused that Iona blew a snort of laughter out her nose, right in his face. "You don't know, do you, sweetheart? You don't know Belinda Beller's boobs are made of paper."

"I don't want to hear you say her name," Willy said.

"Fine," said Iona, breathing in his ear, "I don't wanna talk about her either."

Willy felt the pressure in his crotch, his penis rising against his will. He thought of his mother putting lipstick and rouge on old Mrs. Griswold after she died, but even that didn't help this time.

Iona Moon pounced on top of him, kissing his mouth and locking the door at the same time. She fumbled with his belt, clawed at his zipper. He mumbled *no*, but she smothered the word, swallowed it up in her own mouth.

When Willy wrestled his sisters, his father told him to be careful: The strong have to look out for the weak, he said. It didn't matter that his sisters were older. Even if they jumped him two at a time, Willy was the one who had to go easy. He wasn't strong enough to win a fight without hurting them, without kicking and wrenching and taking a few blind swings, so he had to hold back. Most times he was lucky just to get away.

Willy clamped Iona's arms, but she twisted free. "You know you want it, Willy," she said. "Everybody wants it." But he didn't, not like this, not with Iona

Moon. She bit at his lips and his ears, sharp little nips; her fingers between his legs cupped his balls dangerously tight.

With his hands on her shoulders, he shoved her back, flung her against the dashboard so hard it stunned her, and he had time to unlock the door, leap, and flee. But he didn't get far before he heard the unmistakable sputter of tires in mud, an engine revving, going nowhere. Slowing to a trot, he listened: Rock it, he thought, first to reverse, first to reverse.

He heard her grind through the gears, imagined her slamming the stick, stamping the clutch, thought that by now tears streamed down her hot cheeks. Finally he heard the engine idle down, a pitiful, defeated sound in the near darkness.

Slowly he turned, knowing what he had to do, hearing his father's voice: *A gentleman always helps a lady in distress.* She's no lady. *Who are you to judge?*

He found small dead branches and laid them under the tires in two-foot rows. One steady push, his feet braced against a tree, one more, almost, third time's charm, and the front tires caught the sticks, spun, spat up mud all the way to his mouth, and heaved the truck backward onto solid ground. He wiped his hands on his jeans and clumped toward the road.

"Hey," said Iona, "don't you want a ride?" He kept marching. "Hey, Willy, get in. I won't bite." She pulled up right beside him. "It'll take you more than an hour to get home. Your mama will skin you. Now get in. I won't lay a hand on you." He didn't dare look at her. His face felt swollen, about to explode. "What I did before, I didn't mean anything by it. I never would have tried anything if I thought you wouldn't like it. Willy?" He glanced up at her; she seemed no bigger than a child, hanging on to that huge steering wheel. "Willy, I got a gun. Right here behind the seat, I got my daddy's gun." *Don't you be gettin' any ideas of makin' like a jackrabbit, boy.* Willy didn't know if Iona meant it as a warning or a threat, but he knew there was nothing real behind her words, no reason not to get in the truck, no reason except his pride, and that seemed like a small thing when he weighed it against the five-mile trek along the winding road, his mother's pinched face, and the spot of grease from her nose on the windowpane.

White Falls sat in a hollow, a fearful cluster of lights drawn up in a circle for the night, a town closed in on itself. Iona said, "I almost died once. My brother Leon and I started back from town in a storm that turned to a blizzard. Everything was white, like there was nothing in the world besides us and the inside of this truck. Leon drove straight into a six-foot drift; it looked just the same as the sky and the road. We had to get out and walk, or sit there and freeze like the damn cows. We stumbled, breaking the wind with our hands; then we crawled because the gusts were less wild near the ground. I saw the shadows of houses wavering in the snow, right in front of us, but they were never there. A sheet of ice built up around my cheek and chin, and I kept stopping to shatter it with my fist, but it took too long; Leon said, leave it, it will stop the wind. I thought they'd find me that way, the girl in glass, and they'd keep me frozen in a special truck, take me from town to town along with the nineteen-inch man and the two-headed calf. But Leon, Leon never thought for a minute we were going to die on that road. When I dropped to my belly and said I was warm now, he swatted my butt. Not this way, he said, not this way, God. And then I wondered if he'd whispered it or if I heard what he was thinking. Leon talking to God, I thought; that was more of a miracle than surviving, and I scrambled back to my knees and lunged forward.

"Just like a dog, Leon knew his way. I forgave him for everything. I swore in my heart I'd never hold a harsh thought against him, not for anything in the past or anything he might do later on, because right there in that moment, he was saving our lives.

"When Mama wrapped my hands in warm rags and my daddy pulled off my boots to rub my toes as hard as he could, I knew that nothing, nothing in the world was ever going to matter so much again." She punched the clutch and shifted into fourth. "Do you know why I'm telling you this?" Willy nodded, but he didn't know; he didn't know at all.

It wasn't until Iona Moon eased into her driveway and shut off the engine that she remembered her mother's chocolate and the ragged dollar bill still crumpled in her pocket. *I think I've got to have some pleasure*, that was the last thing Mama said. She rested her head on the steering wheel. A single sob erupted, burst from between her ribs as if someone had pounded his fist against her chest. She fought her own cry, choked it dry, and was silent.

Repentance

*M*Y GREAT AUNT EDITH is visiting from California. She weighs two hundred and thirty pounds and has a dark, golden tan. Her hair is wavy and white and very short. Even though her fingers are crippled from arthritis, like Grandma's, she can still deal a mean hand of cards. She whips me at casino and trounces me at gin. I say, "Let's play fish," and despite the fact that she's never played my game before, it only takes her a few minutes to put me away.

Aunt Edith looks at Grandma, her sister, and says to me, "Why don't you play with Liddy? Maybe you can beat her." Then she laughs, but my grandmother doesn't even know she's been insulted. She thinks it's a good idea, so I humor her. She spreads her cards on the table and I have to show her the moves. This is no game, just something to do with our hands, but Aunt Edith still gets a big kick out of it when Grandma's side wins, and I feel lousy.

Around lunchtime, I tell Aunt Edith I'm going for a walk. I have other plans, but I don't want to tell her about them. Sometimes it's good to keep a secret. Usually I have to stay with Grandma if Mom's not around, because Grandma can't be left alone, even for an hour, so I'm glad Aunt Edith is staying with us, and I figure she can laugh at me all she wants. Mom is glad too, because she gets a day to herself. She and her friend Arvonne drove up to Renton, twenty miles away, to shop. I can't remember the last time Mom did anything like that on the spur of the moment.

I've packed a lunch for myself and hidden it in the hallway. I grab it on my way out the door and yell, "Good-bye, Aunt Edith, good-bye, Gram." I wheel my bike around the back so Aunt Edith won't know I'm riding, not walking like I said. There's no reason to do all this. I feel a little silly, sneaking around, but I do it anyway. Delana, my best friend, is waiting at the appointed place and we pedal our bikes out of town as fast as we can. The hill to the cemetery isn't steep, but it's long. At the top, we spread out a cloth and collapse. The wind is hot and dry and whips our hair into our mouths as we eat our sandwiches.

We hop on our bikes and coast down the road to the

edge of the graveyard where all the children are buried in a special place. An archway marks the entrance with the word BABYLAND spelled out in rusty wire. Delana and I read the stones. One baby lived two months, another almost a year. We stare at a grave where the child didn't even make it through the day, and there is only his name and a single date.

Delana says, "I think it's a waste of time to name a kid if it's born dead."

I say, "How else will his parents find him in Heaven?"

"What do you think they do in Heaven? Keep a register?" says Delana. "You think you walk up to a desk like in a big hotel and say, 'Excuse me, can you tell me where I might find Christopher John Daley?' "

I have to admit it sounds pretty ridiculous if you look at it that way, so I don't bother to tell Delana what I have believed ever since I was six and my grandfather died. I knew that Heaven was eternal and that all the good people who had ever lived were in Heaven now, so it must be getting mighty crowded. I asked my mother, "How will we find Grandpa?" I imagined walking around Heaven for years and years just trying to track down the few people we really loved. Mom lifted me up into her lap and told me not to worry. She said, "When you get to where Grandpa is, all you'll have to do is whisper his name and he'll be right there beside you." The same year, my father moved away and I didn't see him alive again, so of course I thought it was important to know a person's name, even the name of a little baby who never took a breath.

My father and my grandfather and all the relatives I didn't know are buried on the far slope of this cemetery, but I've never told Delana that, or taken her up there. She moved to Tacoma from Chicago two years ago, so no one important to her is in this place.

Grandpa died of lung cancer in his own bed. He and Grandma didn't believe in doctors. They thought sickness formed in the mind and it was up to a man to heal himself, starting with his soul. Toward the end, when it hurt the most, Grandpa must have known the sickness was deep in his body, but Grandma wasn't one to give up. She kept expecting him to wake up some morning feeling fine and saying, "I think I'll plant a few tomatoes today." That's why she couldn't get over the fact that he left her. She thought it was deliberate, I guess, a mean thing.

At first, Grandma was forgetful: she'd forget to get dressed or forget to eat. That wasn't unnatural, but later she seemed to forget Grandpa, refusing to say his name, or answer letters from his sisters. It was her way of paying him back. It took a few years of forgetting before she got to the point where she couldn't remember things even if she tried and then she had to move in with us because she couldn't get out of a chair by herself, or out of bed, or off the toilet. A stiff mind affects the body after a while; she and Grandpa had been right about that connection.

Life was simpler with Grandma right there in the house: we didn't have to check on her all the time, or lug her meals across town. There was plenty of room, since my father had gone to Alaska to work on the pipeline. At least once a day, Grandma said, "Marry in haste, repent at leisure." I knew no facts, but I took that to mean Mom hadn't taken her time to think things through before she married my dad. Maybe they weren't ever that happy together—I honestly couldn't remember. There was no talk of his coming home, even to visit, but he and Mom didn't bother to get divorced, which is why he's buried in the family plot next to Grandpa.

Two months after Grandma moved in with us, we got word my father was lost in a blizzard and had frozen to death. Hearing that he died that way, lost and alone, with the wind throwing snow in his face so it stung like a thousand invisible needles, was a terrible thing, and I realized deep down I hadn't given up the hope that he'd come home and live with us someday when the pipeline was finished. He was coming home, all right, but it wasn't what I'd had in mind.

I shivered, day and night for a week, and had to sleep under a mound of blankets. I just couldn't stop thinking of him in the storm, getting colder and colder. Mom tried to pull some of the covers off me when she thought I was asleep, but as soon as she'd left my room, I'd huddle back under my pile of wool and down.

I might never have stopped feeling like I was freezing if we hadn't gotten this letter from a man who worked with my dad:

Dear Mrs. Nyles,

I know you must think it is an awful thing to die the way your husband died but that is how it goes up here and I just want to tell you it is not so bad, like going to sleep and the cold only bothers you a little at first and then you get very tired and close your eyes. When we found your husband he was curled up and smiling and I swear to you he looked like a little boy having a good dream. Do not think I say this just to be nice. I do not even know you and you do not know me and I have no reason to write except to tell you the truth which is what I am doing.

Very truly yours,
Danny Madsen

I guess Mom and I both trusted Danny Madsen because he really didn't have a reason to lie to us. Maybe I should have been more unhappy that my dad was dead and not just out of town for a bit, but it didn't change anything in my life. In fact, I missed him less than I had when he first left. We got Grandma all dressed up and took her to the funeral with us. When she saw my father lying in his casket, she said, "You make your bed, you have to lie in it." I figured she thought this was the price my father had to pay for walking out on me and my mom and my sister.

Delana knows my father is dead, but she hasn't asked me how it happened or when. Her father is young and very handsome and it probably seems like an impossible idea to her, or just one of those things she doesn't care to imagine. I don't mind. I don't like explaining the whole thing.

I take Delana to the fairy steps that lead to the river. To get there, we have to walk past the mausoleum, where the Bradleys are kept in caskets above the ground. They donated the site for this cemetery, and the woods for our city park. Their mansion is a historical landmark now and that's why they get this little house at the edge of the cemetery. Delana and I grab on to the metal gates that guard the windows and pull ourselves up to look inside, but it's dark and there's nothing to see.

Each fairy step is a rough stone only a few inches wide. We have to walk on tiptoe, like fairies. Along the way, there are benches made from flat slabs of granite. Delana starts to sit on one and I tell her, "Don't do that. This is where the dead people come in the afternoon to sit in the sun and there are probably three or four of them sitting there right now." I'm only teasing her, but Delana is frightened and won't go another step, so we hike back to our bikes and ride home. At the corner where she turns and I go straight, I yell, "See you tomorrow!" She doesn't answer me or turn around to wave. She's mad about that stupid thing with the ghosts, but I don't care.

I guess maybe I did it on purpose, knowing how easy it is to scare Delana.

When I get home, Grandma is hunched in her gold chair, holding a mirror right up to her face and plucking out her whiskers with a pair of tweezers. I ask her, "Where's Aunt Edith?" Grandma doesn't know. I call and call, but Aunt Edith doesn't answer. Finally, I find her, asleep, in the guest room. Her fat, brown hand dangles over the edge of the bed.

In the kitchen, all four gas burners are aflame and I know Grandma wandered around the house doing her mischief after Aunt Edith went down for her nap. If Mom and I are home, Grandma always needs a boost to get her out of her chair. She uses a metal walker to shuffle from one room to another. It gives her four extra feet and makes her good and steady. She can't move a step without it if anyone's watching; but sometimes, when she thinks she's alone, I see her strolling down the hallway with that walker lifted three inches off the ground.

I go back to the living room and am glad to see Grandma has given up on her whiskers. My stomach feels funny when I see her go at her face that way. I say, "Doing some cooking while I was out, Grandma?" Of course she doesn't catch my meaning so I accuse her: "You turned on all the burners."

"No, I didn't," she says.

"Well, someone did," I say, "and I wasn't here and Aunt Edith's asleep, so that leaves you."

"Why would I do that?" she says.

"That's what I'm wondering." I don't know why I'm being so mean. I tell myself that I'm just trying to snap her out of her forgetfulness, but my real intentions are nothing so nice as that.

"You know I can't get up by myself," she says.

"Yeah, right." I stomp out of the room, but in a little while I make her a cup of strong, black tea with milk because I know she likes that in the afternoon. Her hair is full and dark and I brush it for her, hoping that by the time Mom gets here it will have slipped Grandma's mind that I was nasty when I came home.

Mom's been gone only half a day, but I look out the window every five minutes, and when I finally spot the green Dodge I am unreasonably relieved. Arvonne is still with her. Arvonne's nails are so long they've started to curl at the ends. She paints them different colors every week, weird colors like a cold metallic blue, and a brilliant purple. Her hair color changes a lot too and she smokes those long, skinny cigarettes with flowers drawn on the paper. It makes me mad that Arvonne's the one who gets a day alone with Mom. Before Grandma moved in with us, Mom worked days as a switchboard operator, but now she works nights so that one of us is always home with Grandma. The last time I remember having Mom all to myself was May, two years ago. We walked to the wooded park down the street. The cottonwoods were shedding huge flakes of fluffy snow, but it was a warm evening. That made us laugh, and without saying a word, Mom and I both started running, leaping in the air, grabbing at the cotton. Mom is small and pretty. All it takes is something surprising to make her look like she's just a kid, but nothing of the kind has come along for a while.

Arvonne says good-bye outside the house. She gives Mom a big smooch on the cheek, gets in her little Volkswagen, revs it up and peels out. When Mom comes inside, I can see the mark of Arvonne's thin, red lips on her face. Grandma says, "Marg'ret brushed my hair, isn't that sweet?" She always pronounces my name that way, without the middle syllable.

"She's a good girl," Mom says.

"And she made me my tea." Grandma feels fine. The strong tea makes her more alert. I am a cheat and a liar, a bad girl with the wits to do small good deeds.

My sister Maureen and her husband come over later for dinner. Aunt Edith is sluggish from her nap and isn't talking as much as usual. Her white hair is flat on one side and her cheek is creased where she pressed it against a wrinkle in the pillowcase. I put my hand on the table and start to show Maureen how I can bend my knuckles, even the first ones, so my hands look crippled like Grandma's and Aunt Edith's. Maureen slaps my hand and gives me a swift kick under the table before anyone else sees what I'm doing. She's ten years older than I am and thinks that gives her the right to act like she's a mother instead of a sister.

Grandma scrapes the silverware on her plate, waiting for dinner to appear. She's not impatient, just absentminded. My brother-in-law, Roland, looks like he's going to bust when Grandma starts banging her knife and fork together. Mom yells, "I'm coming! I'm coming!" Roland gets a jab from Maureen and does his best to straighten up, but she sees a trace of his silly smirk and gives him a good one in the shin. I think of Grandma's proverbs and wonder if Roland will regret marrying my sister in haste. I imagine them on the porch in early summer the year they graduated from high school. Maureen flips off one sandal, exposing the high arch of her little foot. Roland, studying that perfect foot, is dazed. He means to say, "I want you," but instead he says, "I want to marry you." Because of his proper upbringing, he believes he means the words he's spoken.

After dinner, Maureen has a surprise. She's drawn a picture of Grandma. Every line of Grandma's face is faithfully recorded. The hair is coarse as wire. Beneath the thick glasses, Grandma's eyes are blurred, and the gnarled hands in her lap are lifeless, like birds with broken wings. But there is something tender about the drawing, and I am suddenly aware that Maureen loves my grandmother as I never have. She told me once that Grandma wore real silk stockings and good black shoes every day of her life before she got sick. This memory is important to Maureen and she wants me to see Grandma that way too, but I only see her as she is now, in the drawing, wearing those fuzzy pink slippers. To Maureen, the picture is sad, but to me, it's just Grandma.

For dessert, Grandma eats five or six pinwheel cookies, the big sweet marshmallow ones, covered with chocolate. She weighs eighty-nine pounds and is always hungry, but no matter how much she eats, she can't gain an ounce. Aunt Edith eats a fresh orange instead of cookies. In fact, I haven't seen her eat much at all since she came to visit. Some things don't make sense.

Grandma says to my mother, "Aren't you going to feed me tonight, Eleanor?" She's forgotten the roast beef and beets and mashed potatoes we had two hours ago. She's even forgotten half a dozen pinwheel cookies.

"We just had a big dinner a couple of hours ago," Mom says.

"Not me," says Grandma. "You didn't call me."

Mom points to the table. "You sat right there." She's almost yelling.

Grandma stares at her lap and shakes her head. "No, Eleanor," she says, "no, I certainly didn't."

"Well I'll warm something up for you if you're hungry again," Mom says. She emphasizes the word "again," but otherwise she keeps her voice even.

"No," Grandma says, "that's all right. I'll just go to bed." She sounds so pathetic even I feel a little sorry for her.

Mom says it's no trouble, but Grandma won't take any kindness from her now. Mom's more frustrated by the second and Grandma looks more abused. I don't know what to do, but Maureen saves the day. She goes over and sits on the arm of Grandma's chair and hugs Grandma's rigid, bony shoulders. "Can I make a milkshake for you, Gram?" she says. "A chocolate one, with a banana?" Her voice is as sweet as her offer.

Grandma wants to refuse, to bask in her suffering and accuse us all of neglect, but the milkshake sounds too delicious to pass up, so she says, "Well, all right, yes, that would be nice, Maureen."

Mom's face is so red she has to go into the bathroom for a minute. It's the only room in the house that locks. Roland has been dozing on the couch after dinner, but somehow he wakes up in time to hear the talk about milkshakes, so he calls to Maureen, "Make one for me too, will you, honey?"

Roland pets Maureen's dark, glossy hair as they walk to their car and she turns her cheek upward to him for a kiss. Pretty girls can get away with kicking their husbands, I decide.

I put Grandma to bed because I can see Mom's in no mood for it. After I have tucked her in, I hear Mom talking to Aunt Edith in the kitchen. The kettle whistles. Mom says, "She thinks I'd starve her." The TV is on in the dark living room and I turn it down a notch.

"You can't take these things too seriously, Eleanor," says Aunt Edith. "She's not herself anymore."

"Sometimes I'm cross with her."

"That's understandable."

"I can't help it. I try to hold back, but she knows and then she's off for the whole day. Nothing I do can make it up."

"You're a good daughter to take your mother in the way you have. Not everyone would."

"I told her I hated her once. I ran up the stairs and shouted down at her. For the life of me I can't remember what got me so riled, but I sure remember saying it. I was about Margaret's age."

"Every girl gets upset with her mother now and then," says Aunt Edith. "It's a natural thing."

"My girls never said anything like that to me," says Mom.

I creep closer to the kitchen doorway, thinking of the night Mom told Maureen to hold off a bit with Roland, to give it some time, make sure she had the right man. And Maureen fired right back, "What would you know about finding 'the right man'?"

Aunt Edith says to Mom, "I don't believe it, there isn't a daughter born who doesn't feel the need to blow up at her mom sooner or later. You've forgotten, that's all, just like your mother has forgotten the day you yelled that you hated her. It was forty years ago. Give yourself a break once in a while."

I stand, unseen, in the living room, watching my mother and Aunt Edith under the dingy yellow light of the kitchen. Mom leans over in her chair and rests her head on the gentle slope of Aunt Edith's huge breasts. Aunt Edith puts her arms around Mom and pats her back. This is awkward for Aunt Edith because her arms are so fat and so heavy: they don't fit easily around another person. She looks like a great, brown bear and my mother looks like a lost child.

On Friday, Aunt Edith heads back for California. I think she came here because she thought Grandma was going fast, but Aunt Edith can't wait around forever, so she gives up and goes home.

I pleaded with Mom, "Let me have Delana over to spend the night." Finally she gives in, but she makes me promise to be extra good and extra careful because she doesn't think I should have friends over when she's not home. Delana's parents don't mind because they've never seen my grandmother and Delana tells them Grandma looks after us when my mom's at work. Grandma thinks she really does take care of me, since I'm twelve and she's eighty-three. As Mom goes out the door, Gram says, "Don't worry, I'll watch out for Marg'ret." I look at her eyes behind her thick glasses. They're sunk deep in the sockets, like she's pulling everything a long way inside herself and holding on tight. I imagine her, watching over me with those eyes, following me from room to room, or just knowing what I'm up to even if she sits right there in her chair. Lots of times I think Grandma knows about me, the bad thoughts that go through my head. She can't think straight in the usual way, but I don't believe that necessarily prevents a person from being wise to other kinds of things.

At about seven o'clock, I close the drapes so the living room is dark. Delana should be here any minute and I have to work fast. I tell Grandma it's almost ten. I say, "Aren't you tired?"

"I must be if it's that late," she says.

I think, Someday I'll have to pay for lying to an old woman, for stealing three hours here, an hour there, but I don't worry about it too much tonight because all I really care about is getting her to bed before Delana knocks. Delana doesn't like to see Grandma after Grandma takes her teeth out and puts them in a glass of blue water in the bathroom, and Delana doesn't like to catch a glimpse of my grandmother after she's taken off her robe, either. Old people give her the willies, she says.

I help Grandma out of her chair, putting one hand in her armpit and the other beneath her forearm. The loose flesh slips around the bone.

She takes a long time in the bathroom and I pace the hallway. Delana is late already. Any second she'll be at the door, but no matter how slow Grandma is in the bathroom, I won't help her there.

Grandma appears at last, disoriented, almost blind without her glasses. She's stooped and small. She needs me and doesn't pretend it's the other way around. In the old pictures I've seen, my grandmother is tall. The bones of her hips pierce the lines of her silk dresses but she is not skinny. She looks sturdy. She looks a bit like me:

narrow in the shoulders, but broad in the hips, a girl
with a long, thin nose and big hands.

I pull the covers up to her chin, kiss her good-night,
and tell her I love her. I leave her one line of light as I
close the door, but she pleads, "Not too far," so I open it
one inch more.

Delana taps on the window. We go right to the basement, to the room that's been mine since Maureen got
married and moved out. Mom can't understand why both
of us like that dark, damp room best of all. The windows
near the ceiling are old and unclean. Mom says it's de-
pressing and she doesn't even like to come downstairs.
That's just fine with me.

There are games I play with Delana and no one else.
I call her my best friend, but in fact she's my only friend.
Tonight, we take turns pretending we are captors.
Delana tells me a story while she ties me up: she's kidnapped me because my father owns an oil company and
she wants to collect a huge ransom. I slip out of Delana's
knots in three minutes flat and tell her she can forget
getting any money from my father.

Now I get my chance with her. This is the story I
tell her: I am a man who has been terribly disfigured in
a fire and has never had love because of it, and never
sought love, but I have fallen in love with her against my
will and I've taken her captive to teach her to love me
despite my ugliness. I promise to let her go as soon as I

can trust her. Delana's an odd choice for this madness, I admit. She's not the kind of girl who would make any man do a crazy thing. To begin with, she's short and skinny. Her arms are covered with freckles, her eyes are brown as beans, and she has a quick, nervous way of moving that makes the kids at school call her "bird girl." But the man I've become finds her beautiful.

I don't have a real closet, just a small alcove with an Indian bedspread hung like a curtain in front of it, but I tell her it's a closet and I put a chair in there and tie her to it. Delana grunts in the dark. We have a rule in this game—we can't talk and we can't yell. The legs of the chair thump up and down like she's trying to make it walk out of the closet. I know she's not making any progress with the ropes, but I don't let her out, not right away, because that's not the agreement and she wouldn't let me out if things were reversed.

Even though I'm all the way downstairs, I hear Grandma calling, "Eleanor, Eleanor." I've learned to hear every sound she makes no matter where I am in the house. I leave Delana tied behind the curtain while I go to try to get Grandma back to bed. As I walk down the hallway, Grandma's door creaks open and she says, "Eleanor? Is that you?"

"It's me, Gram," I say, "it's Margaret. Mom's gone out for the night. Go back to bed." She waits by the door. She won't go to bed by herself. I have to tuck her in again, and kiss her again. Her mouth seems to fall into itself and her lips curve around the ridge of her gums.

She hasn't had teeth for nearly forty years. Mom told me she had a gum disease and all her teeth were pulled at once. Her face was swollen and bruised and she couldn't talk or eat for days. That's why I try not to look at Grandma's mouth when her teeth are in the bathroom. I don't like to think about it.

I sit on the edge of her bed. "Marg'ret," she says, "is it almost morning?"

"No, Grandma, you just got in bed. Go back to sleep."

"Marg'ret?" she says as I go to the door, "Will your mother be home soon?"

"Yes, Gram, very soon." I try to sound patient, to reassure her.

I grab a paper bag and hurry back downstairs, remembering Delana's still tied in the closet. I didn't bother to tell her I heard Grandma calling—I just left.

I poke two holes in the paper bag and put it over my head. Delana's all sweaty and straining against the ropes. She's worked her way half out of the closet, but she can't get free of the bedspread. As I pull the curtain back, I say, "I don't want to scare you with my face, so I've covered it. If I untie you, do you promise not to run away?" For a few more minutes I want to be the horrible man who has fallen helplessly in love with Delana.

"No," she says, "I won't promise."

I let the curtain drop around her. "Then I can't untie you," I say.

"Knock it off, Margaret. My wrists hurt."

Calling me by my real name means the game is over, but I untie her slowly, leaving the paper bag over my face. I tell her she owes me one for being so nice and untying her and all when she won't promise to be a good girl. She shivers like an unbroken pony about to be mounted. When I slip the last rope off her wrist, she stands up, spins around, belts me hard in the gut and says, "There, that's the one I owe you. Now we're even."

I say, "That didn't hurt," but I'm almost gagging for those first few breaths. I laugh as soon as I can and act like it's no big deal 'cause I don't want Delana to get mad and go home.

Mom gets off work at eleven, but it's after midnight and she's not home yet. I figure she must have gone out for a drink with Arvonne. They work the same shift and it's Friday, after all.

Delana and I bring the TV downstairs and lie stretched in front of it with the sound turned off and the pictures flickering like blue flames. We are playing the operation game. Delana has her tools ready: a pencil, a pair of scissors, a wet rag. First she washes my arm with the rag. She speaks in a low voice, to comfort me. "Don't be afraid," she says, "this won't hurt much. I'm just cleaning up your arm now to prevent infection." With the pencil she marks the place where the incision must be made. During the past few months, Delana and I have operated on each other's faces and necks, backs and thighs.

The light strokes of the pencil tickle and I clench my fist, trying not to giggle. Delana says, "Relax, you have to relax." Her mouth is right up close to my ear and she rubs my arm with her cool hand so that I'll be still.

Now she is ready to make the incision. She opens the scissors and draws them along the same places she marked with the pencil. Each time she does it she presses a little harder. She talks to me while she scratches. Her hot breath is in my face. The scissors hurt a little more each time and I think I won't be able to stand it any longer, but I do because I don't want her to stop talking. "Take it easy," she says. "Remember, this is for your own good." I start to feel I really have been drugged for an operation and I float above myself, watching, then the blade of the scissors doesn't sting at all. That's when I hear Grandma call my name.

The incision is complete. "Now I'm going to peel the skin back," says Delana. She tugs at my arm, pretending to have a rough time with this task. When she finally says, "Aaah, I have it," I swear it prickles as if the skin is being pulled from the flesh. Suddenly, every sensation is sharp in that one place, like all the nerves have come alive and the rest of my body has gone to sleep. Delana prods and pokes, searching for imaginary tumors. Grandma calls again. Her voice is louder now, as if she is closer. Each time Delana finds one of these tumors, she plucks it out quickly, pinching me. She is making a pile beside us. I think I should go see what Grandma needs, but I don't want to move. This operation feels too good, and too strange. My whole body seems to vibrate slightly: there's a low hum deep inside my bones. Even if I stood up to go to Grandma, I'm not sure I could walk.

"You're a lucky girl," says Delana. "I think I got them all. I'll just close you up now." She pulls the skin back over the opening and starts to sew. Her needle must be the pencil, but my eyes are closed and I won't open them because it will all be over if I can see that none of it was real. Grandma calls once more, first my name, then Mom's. Even Delana hears her this time. She doesn't say it, but I can tell because she starts stitching faster.

When Grandma yells, "Marg'ret? Are you there?" for the fourth time I can't ignore her. She sounds frightened and she's close enough for me to hear the *click-click* of her walker. I jerk my arm away from Delana. Jumping up too fast makes me dizzy, but I make a run for it anyway.

The light in the living room, behind Grandma, outlines her frail silhouette at the top of the stairs. She can't see me. "Don't move, Grandma," I say, "stay right there." The walker falls first, bouncing down the stairway banging from wall to wall. I have to leap out of its path, so I don't see Grandma fall, but I hear the soft thud of her body; I count the steps she hits, three, four.

I fling the walker out of my way and practically fly up the stairs. She hasn't fallen far, and is just sitting there as if nothing's wrong and she meant to do it.

"Why didn't you answer me?" Grandma says.

I say, "I was asleep." This is my worst lie, because

it matters. "Are you all right?" I say. At first I think she looks all right, but then I notice her left arm is twisted back in a way that can't be natural and I know enough not to try to move her.

Delana crouches at the bottom of the stairs. "Come here," I say. My voice is loud and rough. Delana does what I say. "Stand here," I say, pointing to the stair I'm on, "and watch her. I have to call an ambulance."

She climbs to the step below me and stares at my grandmother's mouth. She won't move any closer. I make the call and come back to sit on the stairs with Grandma. She says, "I called and called. I thought you'd gone off and left me."

"I didn't hear you," I say. "I was asleep." The lie is more comfortable the second time. Delana doesn't make a beep, but she glares at me like I might be the lowest thing that ever crawled the earth.

Mom pulls in the driveway almost the same time the ambulance arrives and Arvonne is close behind in her noisy little Volkswagen. Before Mom even gets in the house, she figures out what has happened and heads straight for the stairs. She flicks on the light above us. Grandma and Delana and I all sit there, blinking.

Arvonne peers over my mother's shoulder and swears a few times in a row, softly, so the words are just hisses between her teeth. Mom doesn't say anything. She studies us. Grandma is alive and doesn't look too bad. The ambulance is here and there's no reason to get worked up.

The two men shoo me and Delana out of the way so they can work. We scuttle to the bottom of the stairs; Mom and Arvonne wait at the top. With the slant of the stairs, it's a tricky business getting Grandma on the stretcher, but it takes less than a minute. Under her breath, Delana whispers, "You should have gone the first time she called." I don't answer Delana. I don't even bother to look at her.

I follow the men, but Delana stays behind. Grandma is babbling now, like something got knocked loose in her head when she fell. She says, "Well, at last you're home, Eleanor. I told you not to stay out past dark. Now you've missed dinner. I want you home right after school every day this week, young lady, and no argument."

Mom says, "No, Mama, no argument." Mom snaps and unsnaps the clasp on her purse. Turning to Arvonne, she says, "I knew I shouldn't go out for a drink. I knew it. I told you. Didn't I say, 'I have a feeling I should go home?' Didn't I say that?"

"Yeah," says Arvonne, "and I told you to forget it. You always have a feeling." She sounds as miserable as my mom and they both smell like they've had three or four beers, not one or two.

We go outside, trotting behind the men to watch them lift Grandma into the ambulance. They are so careful, almost tender, and I'm grateful. I tell myself, "She's all right now. Everything's all right. They'll take care of her."

In the confusion of it all, Mom has forgotten I'm there, but before she climbs into the ambulance to sit with Grandma, she takes my face in her hands and says, "You're a good girl. Were you scared, baby? You did all the right things, just right. You're Mom's good girl."

When she says that, I wish a hole would open where I stand so that I could sink straight down and disappear. I expected questions: Where were you? What were you doing? How could you let this happen? I expected to lie, again, but she assumes I was asleep, assumes I didn't hear Grandma until it was too late. My only lie is not telling her the truth.

Arvonne says, "Yeah, you're a cool-headed one, all right." It sounds like a compliment, but coming from Arvonne, I know it means she thinks there's something wrong with a kid who stays calm in a situation like this. Eyeing Arvonne's green fingernails, I think if anyone could spot a fraud, it would be Arvonne. She drives off to meet my mother at the hospital and I keep sight of her red taillights until she turns, a quarter mile up the road.

Delana has finally come outside and we both stay in the driveway, but we stand apart. She is crying, or pretending to cry. I walk toward her. I don't see any real tears. She says, "I want to go home." I tell her to shut up. I tell her she can't go home because there's no one to drive her and I won't let her walk home in the dark.

After that night, Delana and I aren't friends anymore. She tells the other kids at school how I was mean to my grandmother, how I teased her and ignored her. She says she begged me to go help Grandma, but I wouldn't, and she was too scared to do it herself. The way Delana tells the story, I might as well have had my hands on Grandma's back and shoved her down the stairs.

I start to wonder: maybe Grandma's falling is my punishment for a lot of things. I think about the games with Delana, the thrill of tying her up, and later the operation, how distracted I was, Delana's slender fingers, Delana's breath and her face above me, blue from the light of the TV. When we played these games, I always listened for the sound of footsteps, or a door opening. I knew I didn't want to get caught, but I didn't know why.

I am afraid of my grandmother now, though she does nothing but lie in her bed at the hospital. Each time we visit, I imagine she'll suddenly have the strength to rise up and accuse me, point her crooked finger and rail at me for all of my evils against her. She'll tell my mother how I pretended I didn't hear her call that night, and it was not the first time. She'll expose my trick of closing the drapes and telling her it was time for bed. Perhaps she'll even recall the day Delana and I put on masks and danced and whooped outside the front window, taunting her, until she was in such a frenzy that she lifted her walker and shook it at us. Her glasses slipped, the combs fell loose from her hair; still we carried on that way and never showed our faces.

But Grandma does not reveal my wickedness. She is

very sick. At first, the doctor tells us only her arm is broken, but every day, when the nurse lifts her onto the bedpan, Grandma moans as if she's being tortured. Every day, the nurse says, "This woman has a broken hip." The doctor denies it. On the third day, the nurse, a thick, ruddy woman with stubby fingers, puts her hands on her hips and refuses to move my grandmother again until she's been x-rayed. The nurse is right, of course. She's lifted enough old women to recognize a broken hip.

Maureen tries to visit her at mealtimes so she can feed Grandma and keep her company while she eats. Maureen lifts the spoon and tells Grandma to open up. She calls her "my little bird" and Mom and I leave the room.

Each day, I am afraid Grandma will be dead. Each day, I am afraid she will start to get well and the doctor will tell us she can leave the hospital soon. In a dream, Grandma waits till she is home to confront me. We are alone and she says she knows what Delana and I were doing that night. She knows why I didn't come when she called. She laughs at me. Her mouth opens wide so I can see her pink tongue, waggling. She calls me a sinful girl and I know I will be repenting as long as I live. Only my servitude will buy her silence. But the dream ends with the clatter of the walker in the stairwell. This is what I always see, last of all.

Nothing like this happens. Grandma is lost. The white walls of the hospital, the white sheets, the white gown she wears, have totally befuddled her. To her, this must be like a blizzard. She goes in circles, as my father did. She gives up, and closes her eyes, and waits.

Aunt Edith flies up from California and we drive straight to the hospital. Grandma knows Aunt Edith right away and looks sharper than she has in days, but she doesn't know me or Mom. She says, "Who are these pretty little girls you've brought to see me?"

Later that night Mom and I sit in the kitchen. She makes fairy tea for both of us, one dunk of the tea bag, the palest green possible. She says, "I can't get over it," and I know she is thinking about Grandma not recognizing her. Often Grandma doesn't know me, or the doctor, or Maureen, but she has always known Mom. Even when she is too tired to open her eyes or talk, she hears Mom's voice and smiles.

Mom tells me she has been having dreams about losing all her teeth. Her jaw is stiff and sore. She says, "As soon as I wake up, I put my fingers in my mouth to feel my teeth." She makes me promise to tell her if I ever see a whisker on her face.

I stop dreaming about Grandma reviling me. I dream that I stand in front of my mother and she says she doesn't know who I am.

Grandma lingers as the snow piles up inside her head, seeing less and less in her white world. She curls into herself and finally slips away.

*   *   *

Maureen wears a dove-gray dress to the funeral and takes
care of greeting the relatives. She is calm and peaceful
and lets everyone kiss her cheek. Mom and I fidget. I
crack my knuckles and Maureen puts her hand over
mine, delicately, as if her hand is a lace handkerchief.
Mom blows her nose about twenty times, but her eyes
are dry. Arvonne keeps my mother under her wing all
day, escorting her from place to place, handing her
Kleenex, patting her arm.

There's a chill wind at the cemetery, though the day
is bright and clear. It's May and the cottonwoods have
shed. Their white fluff skims across the ground. Aunt
Edith sees me shifting from foot to foot, trying to get a
better look at the hole that's waiting. She plops her heavy
hand on my shoulder and says, "You'll miss your grandmother, won't you?" I nod. It is such a small lie after all
the other lies.

At home, I try to sleep. A dozen times in the past
week Mom has said, "I wonder how long she would have
had if I hadn't gone for a drink with Arvonne." She
thinks all the blame is hers because she didn't come
straight home that night, but when she says this, I feel
my crime has doubled. I bear my mother's guilt, and my
own.

I think about the years before Grandma lived with
us, before my father left for Alaska. My mother always
checked on me in the night, covering me up if I'd kicked
the blankets off the bed, or pulling the comforter down if

she put her hand on my head and thought I felt too warm. Sometimes, when Dad's snoring kept her awake, she'd crawl in bed with me and stay till morning.

Now, I hear the whush of her slippers as she scuffles down the hallway, back and forth. She thinks I'm too old for her to check on me, and there's no one left in the house to snore too loudly, no excuse for her to sleep in my bed. I hear the click of the light in the kitchen and, later, the curtains being drawn in the living room. I want to call to her and confess. I want to release her so she knows at last it was not her fault at all. Maybe I just want to sit and talk until it's not so dark. But I don't call. The muscles in my arms and legs are tight and weary; my eyes are open wide. I stay in bed, listening to my mother as she flips the pages of a magazine.

Small Crimes

HE KNEW HE WAS HANDSOME. Years ago, that
is, when he was a struggling poet and an overwrought
advertising hack, churning out copy for products he had
never seen, a man destined to fail at the thing that earned
him money because, he claimed, he gave his heart, his
blood, his sleep to the art that earned him nothing.
Mostly he gave his sleep and polluted his blood, nurtur-
ing shots early in the morning and sucking whiskey
straight from the bottle as dawn threatened. He forgot all
about his heart. That was closer to the truth. And now?
He was no longer handsome. The booze had taken care
of everything the accident had missed. But he was no
longer struggling either. He'd had enough acclaim to find
comfort and respect at various universities along the way.

The guest professor, he liked that. It was a nice role for a man who hadn't finished college. San Francisco was his home this year, and he'd rented a studio with a fireplace in North Beach so he could be right in the middle of things.

Today he was meeting a student for lunch to discuss her work. The only mirror in his apartment was hung safely in the bathroom, so he had plenty of space to imagine himself at thirty, remembering every detail of the picture on the back of his first book. The photograph froze the wild waves of his dark hair and caught one raised brow in a relentless question. A swirl of smoke curled from the full lips, his full lips. He hoped his young lady had seen that photograph.

Their appointment was at noon. He took a swig from the whiskey bottle and chased it with a swallow of mouthwash. The ritual had been repeated several times during the long morning, and each time he'd told himself it was the last. This time he said the words out loud.

Since he knew the girl would be prompt, he waited until ten past twelve to leave for the restaurant. It was just around the corner, on Montgomery, one of those small, perpetually dark places below street level. He hadn't been able to write a word all morning, but he wanted to appear harried and disheveled, as if he had torn himself from the typewriter, from what might be the most brilliant stanza of his career, just to keep his date with her.

It worked beautifully. A cup of coffee was in front

of her already. She wore a white blouse with a high collar
buttoned to the very top. Her long, light hair was swept
from her face and tied loosely with a green ribbon. She
was nervous. The cup jiggled in her hand when she saw
him. She was lovely. She was waiting for him and he
wasn't such an old man.

"Sorry I'm late," he said, pulling out his chair.

"I know you're busy," she said. "It was kind of you
to meet me at all, Mr. Brandon."

"Please. Ted," he said, "call me Ted."

"Ted," she said, so softly and reluctantly that he
could barely keep himself from reaching across the table
and squeezing her hand. He held back. Patience was a
necessity with young girls.

"Have you decided what you want?" he said. She
hadn't. He waved to the waiter. He was a regular customer here, so the boy was attentive. Ted Brandon ordered for both of them. "It's the best thing on the menu,"
he said as the waiter scurried off. "I hope you don't mind
my taking the liberty." She didn't, not at all. He had
made her wait for him and now he had ordered her meal.
Things were nicely under control.

"It's a shame the semester is over," he said. "I've
enjoyed your class, but then what man wouldn't? I felt
blessed every time I walked into class and saw twelve
pretty girls with their legs crossed and their hair curled."
He knew at once he'd said the wrong thing. "And there
was some decent writing in your group too. That's not
always the case." Her lips were tight and she focused on

her cup of coffee where the cream had made the surface oily. He reminded himself to stay alert and be more careful.

"Of course there's no one I admire as a potential equal except for you, Denise." It sounded false, even to him, perhaps because he'd used it too many times in the past, but he half meant it this time, despite his motives. He knew from her poems that her father must have died when she was still young. Brandon saw the man's chapped hands that cracked and bled in the wintertime. Her father stooped to kiss her, scraping his coarse stubble against her cheek until she begged him to stop. Brandon thought he must be a laborer or a farmer. Once he fell asleep in his big leather chair while he was reading her a story, and she sat there in his lap, afraid to wake him, not moving minute after minute. Ted Brandon rarely remembered his students' poetry for more than a week, but this image stuck, and in his mind he saw the wide-open eyes of the blond child as she perched stiffly against her snoring father. It made him uncomfortable in a way, to recall it so vividly.

Those eyes were opened for him now. She wanted to believe he meant what he said. He plunged into it. "There's an honesty in you. You can see yourself as a child, yet you write like a woman." It was the right tone, the proper order.

Her eyes were remarkably green. She was testing him, staring him down to see if he was telling the truth. To blink or move would finish him off in a flash. The ash of his cigarette was so long it was about to fall on his hand. He wanted a drag desperately, but he kept his hands flat on the table and peered back at her until she smiled, exposing the gap between her front teeth. He put the cigarette to his lips and took a long pull.

Ted Brandon could see this was going to be an exhausting afternoon. These young girls required far more flattery than older women did. At forty, a woman knows you're there because it's convenient, possible, and she is neither too ugly nor too boring. A girl in her twenties still values her unique nature and a man must never, never forget to tell her what separates her from all the others.

The food was slow. A silence had to be filled, so he offered her a cigarette. She accepted. That was promising. He couldn't remember ever seeing her smoke. He asked her. No, she said, she didn't smoke, well, occasionally, as he could see. He had her on edge. Yes, the cigarette was a good sign.

He knew she had a boyfriend and he hoped that wouldn't get in the way later on. Ted Brandon had seen her with the young man, and had even gone to the trouble to find out his name: Cristadoro, Michael Cristadoro. He was rather short and had a pockmarked face and bad teeth; but in his first year of graduate school, he'd already established quite a reputation in the Philosophy Department. At the thought of the gifted, unappealing boy, Ted Brandon had to suppress a grin. There was something of the martyr in this elegant girl, something of the savior. He suspected she took pleasure in making a gift of her beauty to a boy who was less fortunate. Well, that was fine with him, just fine.

The waiter served their chicken and it was safe to order wine. He longed for a stiff belt, but it was too early, and he was still concerned with what she thought of him.

Months ago she'd told him she was from Iowa, and he'd worried that her poise was a façade and underneath it all she was really one of those rowdy Midwesterners who tipped over sleeping cows for amusement on Friday nights. Watching her careful bites, he decided she was definitely not that kind. He liked restrained girls. An effusive woman couldn't be trusted.

"Have you read any of my books?" he said. He thought he knew the answer and expected her to say, shyly, "Yes, oh yes, Mr. Brandon—Ted—I admire your work so much." She said nothing. Did she think he was crazy to even ask? Had he offended her? That look, god, he couldn't tolerate it when women studied him that way, a bug on a board with a pin stuck through his middle.

Anne did that to him too, and as long as he lived he could not forget the first night they spent tossing in each other's arms. She'd twisted her auburn hair into one braided coil, so thick and stiff it seemed almost dangerous. He fell asleep on top of her and when she tried to work herself free, the braid slapped against the sheet and he woke with a start, ready to fling it from the bed. She laughed, her girlish whinny. He was groggy and confused; but she was sharp, and looked at him so coolly that he knew at once her eyes had been open all along.

Much later she confessed he was her first and he hadn't taken her over the edge or anywhere near it. She knew so little then. It was enough to be crazy for him, to have already decided she wanted him to marry her. And it was interesting, exactly that, she insisted, to watch his frenzy, to watch his forehead wrinkle till the brows came together, and finally to witness the wet, just-kissed lips twist into a silent, breathless scream, my god, my god, my god.

He wondered if this girl sitting across the table from him would stare at him while they made love. The right side of his face was scarred from the night he went to sleep at the wheel and slammed his new Volkswagen into the median. Half the cheek was a raw pink where the shards of the shattered windshield had torn into his flesh. He was always careful to turn his head slightly when he spoke to people so it wasn't as noticeable. His black hair was gray now, but still thick. The skin below his eyes was purple and slightly swollen. If she had any sense, she'd close her eyes.

Damn it anyway. Just thinking about Anne made him feel like a used-up old fool. Their daughter, Stephanie, was older than this girl he wanted to lure back to his apartment. He knew what she'd think of her father if she could see him now. Stephanie, his striking daughter, had Anne's fair skin and his distinctive brows and dark hair.

But the lithe child had become a chubby adolescent and now she was a heavy woman. That was a polite description. When she let him hug her in their rigid way, he felt the bulge of fat squeezed out beneath the elastic of her bra and he was so sorry for someone. He didn't know if he was sorry for her because she must be unhappy or sorry for himself, because after the divorce, he had always consoled himself with the knowledge he was the father of such a pretty girl, and no matter what Anne took from him, she couldn't take that.

The girl pushed her unfinished lunch away from her, and Brandon made a show of lighting his cigarette. He had the long, limber fingers of a pianist. Each cuticle was a perfect half-moon on a healthy, pink nail—a poet's hands, he thought, flicking his wrist at once to extinguish the match, the hands of a man who works with his brain.

He squinted to take a better look at the girl he had chosen for himself during the very first class. His sense of propriety made him congratulate himself. He had waited for the semester to be over because he was not, after all, one of those professors who took advantage of his students. But it had not been easy to hold back when they were bent over her poems, alone in his office, and he caught a breathful of the clean soapy smell of her hair.

He knew the glow of her skin would fade and in time the lines would expose her true nature. He accepted her innocence as a lie. And he knew that she might have already written her best poems and her talent would come to almost nothing. In ten years she might have lost both charm and promise, but what did that matter to him? He wanted her now. That was his gift. Could she possibly fathom such generosity?

The waiter cleared their plates and offered more coffee to the girl. She said, "Thank you, no," and wiped the corners of her mouth with her napkin. She wasn't wearing any lipstick, but her mouth was very red. She was a rosy girl, nothing like Anne, whose skin was so white and thin that the veins showed through and made her forehead look almost blue sometimes. He reached for the girl's hand.

They'd barely mentioned her work, and that was the reason they'd used to meet for lunch, after all. He turned his clutch into a press of professional support and said, "You're a gifted young lady. You need polish, but you have feeling and control."

It was necessary to be vague. He'd only skimmed the last five poems she'd given him. Admiration could be an interference. He was uneasy. That was wrong. It was supposed to be the other way around: the student should be ill at ease with the poet. He didn't release her hand and he had no intention of doing so. She wouldn't pull away, not now. She had come for this praise, had sat through lunch just to hear these words that he proffered at last with such marvelous restraint. He had to flatter her, and leave her wanting more. He might be old, but Ted Brandon was no fool.

"Your poems about your father are the most powerful," he said. He'd decided to tackle the issue head-on and get it out of the way. "How old were you when he died?"

"He's not dead," said the girl.

"But your poems—I thought . . ."

"Yes?"

"They seem so final."

"I'm not sure I know what you mean," she said.

"Neither am I." Brandon chuckled. There was something terrible about assuming a man was dead when he wasn't. "How old is he?"

"Sixty-two."

Brandon was relieved. He was only fifty-six. This was very important. "But he's a farmer, right?"

"A banker," said the girl, "president of a small bank."

"But his hands—you wrote how they chapped and bled when he worked outside." He was insistent now, almost angry. He felt deceived, no, worse—tricked.

"He's always building something—a shed, a stone path—or shoveling snow without his gloves."

Brandon felt a little better. She had not meant to mislead him.

"A hardy Midwesterner," he said.

"Just oblivious," said the girl.

The check came; and while Brandon fumbled with his money, both he and the girl took the opportunity to let the subject of her father drop.

"I'm such an idiot," Brandon said. "I meant to bring those poems you gave me to lunch. I have a few suggestions. They're so close to being flawless, it's a shame not to give them the finishing touches. Do you have a few minutes? My apartment is just a couple of blocks away."

As they walked he told her how difficult it was to move as often as he had. "I never get to know people well enough to ask them to my apartment. West Coast people are casual on the surface, but I find they keep a proper distance. Being from Iowa, you must have felt it too." Yes, she had. He knew something about her after all. "Everyone meets me for lunch, or cocktails, or comes to my office. It's been so long," he said, "since another person has walked through that oversized room I call an apartment. It will be nice to have you there, Denise." He wanted her to feel honored he'd chosen her. He wanted her to feel a little sorry for him, but he was careful not to make her feel pity. Pity could be the death of every other feeling. He was plotting, but everything he'd said was true, and it would be nice, it would be so nice to have her there.

She stood at the window, looking down at the parking lot three stories below. He stood behind her, holding a cognac for her in one hand and a whiskey for himself in the other. The sky was dark. It was still early, but a hard rain was on its way and the air was heavy. A string of firecrackers burst and children scattered. An engine idled down and a car door slammed. In the quiet that followed, he said her name, set the drinks on the window-sill, and moved as close to the girl as he could without putting his hands on her.

He asked for a kiss. She didn't answer. He wanted to unbutton that blouse of hers and bare her white neck, to kiss her in the hollow where the collarbone forms a delicate ridge on a woman who is neither too fat nor too thin, to put his tongue there in that one place where the skin is more silken than anywhere else on a woman's body.

He wrapped his long arms around her back and she placed her hands firmly on his shoulders to tell him that was all he'd get. He was a tall man who still had some strength. He let her feel it just so she'd know he could take what he wanted if he were that kind of man.

"I'm going to kiss you," he said. "It's been so long I've almost forgotten how a woman tastes. No, I'll never forget. That's the shame. I'll always want it."

"I have a boyfriend," she said, but her voice told him she knew how feeble this excuse was.

"Yes," he said, "and if young Cristadoro ever slips from the saddle . . ."

The allusion made her wince, and for the first time Ted Brandon was weary of her refined manner and simply took what he wanted.

She allowed him to kiss her bright little mouth, but she kept her arms braced on his shoulders and her lips unopened. To reach her, he had to stoop and a hollow gapped between their bodies, a space so wide a child

could have stood in it. How ridiculous they would look
to anyone gazing up from the parking lot, he thought, an
old man bent over a reluctant girl. He released her and
handed her the cognac.

"I should go," she said.

"No," he snapped. How dare she let him kiss her
that way. It was better to shove a man away than to let
the lips lie so still a man felt he must be a ghost, nothing
more to her than a damp wind blowing past her face. He
was a teacher. She was his student. That was all. They'd
met today to discuss poetry. Well, he had something to
tell her, if that's why she was here. He might be a chain-
smoking old whiskey guzzler who was never going to
have a woman again, but he was still a poet, a real poet,
and he had something to offer this girl with too little
experience and too much education.

"You're not a poet yet," he said. "Maybe you never
will be." Her eyes filled but she held back. In seconds he
had obliterated an afternoon of careful praise. What of it,
he thought. She came for flattery. He came for pleasure.
They were both guilty, but the crimes were so small.

"You won't be a poet until something in you dies,
until you're swallowed up and shit out the other end.
And all the poems you write will be your miserable,
futile, puling effort to bring that dead part of yourself
back to life."

"I'm leaving," she said. "I don't have to listen to
this."

"You want to listen," he said. "You want to know

what turned this man into a poet. You'll be the first. How can you resist?"

She sat down in his rigid oak chair with the high back and the hard seat. She was curious or scared. He had an ace in his boot. When nothing else broke a woman down, this did. It meant walking a dangerous line along the edges of fear and pity and repulsion; and if he got the balance wrong, she'd bolt. It meant telling her something that made him too despicable to hate. To make it work, you had to stop caring how it all turned out. Only one story was in his mind, and he had never told it to anyone, even in his most desperate moments. If she fancied herself the savior, he would show her how humiliated and afraid a man could be. He was going to tell her about Colombia, about what had happened almost twenty years ago, because her lifeless lips in his hot mouth made every door in his brain slam shut.

He sat in a chair across the room that was the mate to the girl's chair. He wanted distance now that he'd finally found his audience. The room was gray, darker by the minute, and the first plops of rain hit the roofs of cars and streaked down his windowpanes in slow, muddy rivulets.

"I went to Bogotá after my divorce," he said. "I had been to Colombia once, right after I had dropped out of college, and I remembered it romantically, as a place that was hot and exotic. I hadn't written a single poem since Anne had left me. I thought some sweet *mamacita* might revive me. I spoke a little Spanish, enough to get by.

"I didn't book a return flight. I planned to stay as long as it took. I didn't even know what I meant by that. As long as it took to get over Anne? to be fluent in Spanish? I hadn't decided.

"Within a week I knew I wasn't making progress in any direction. I holed up in my hotel room for days at a time and played back the scenes of my marriage, trying to make them come out another way. The women were a disappointment. Their hips were broad and their breasts sagged from bearing half a dozen children in as many years. Only the young girls with their tight little buttocks gave me occasional distraction. I watched them in the street below my window. Half-hidden by the stained curtains, I worked myself into a frenzy several times a day.

"I imagined their black hair falling against my chest and their thin, brown legs wrapped around my thighs. That was enough at first, and I thought I was too good to pay for a prostitute. But it grew worse and worse; I rubbed myself till I was sore and got no satisfaction, coming on the windowsill, biting the inside of my own cheek. Before long, the rationale came to me quite simply: I considered myself a benefactor. The girl I chose would want me, genuinely, not just for money. But I would give her a small present all the same, enough pesos to buy herself a necklace or a new dress. The transparency of my 'generosity' did not bother me.

"I knew where to go. There were special bars in Bogotá and an American man in a hotel was made aware of these things. I waited till dusk and made my way into the heart of the west end. I tried to look casual, aimless, disinterested, but the young ladies were not deceived; and as I passed by them on the street, they brushed against me, whispering, *'Hola, mi amor.'* I didn't want a streetwalker. One was too skinny, another too dark. I could afford to be choosy.

"I found her in a cramped bar, or, rather, she found me. She called herself Rosa and her lips were full and painted red. Perhaps she was thirteen, but I told myself she was seventeen at least, that these Colombian girls were small for their ages. She had a way of raising one of her heavy eyebrows that made her look wise and cynical beyond her years.

"Her English was better than my Spanish and we closed our deal with a few words. I was no benefactor and she accepted no gifts. As soon as we left the bar, she insisted I give her the money up front, three hundred pesos, about two dollars.

"She told me to follow her. I expected to head down an alleyway and up a flight of stairs, but we walked three blocks and she didn't seem to be slowing her pace. In my gut, I knew something wasn't right. She was taking me too far, into a part of the city I didn't know. The buildings were nothing but shacks and they looked deserted. I hesitated and the girl turned. *'Yo me lo piso,'* she said. My ability to understand Spanish was gone. At first I thought she was asking me for more money. She smiled and beckoned. That eyebrow arched—a challenge. I had already paid her; I kept going. I was too much of a man to admit I'd been duped by a child. Yes, that's how I saw her now, as the child she was, and I wanted to get it over with so I wouldn't have to think about it anymore.

"The streets shrunk to winding paths between huts of cast-off metal and scrap lumber. I ran the words over in my mind—*'Yo me lo piso'*—and decided she'd said something like, 'I want you to give it to me on the floor.' The thought of it was stronger than my disgust or my fear.

"I heard soft thuds on the earth, the sound of distant horses, but in an instant I realized it was the sound of children's bare feet on the dirt and they were running toward me from every side, as if they'd been crouching in the shadows by the shacks, waiting until it was impossible for me to escape.

"They charged me. There were a dozen or so in their gang. None looked older than twelve and one or two looked as young as six. Rosa crossed her arms over her thin chest and watched. Switches and sticks were their only weapons. You can see I'm a big man and I was young and strong then. At first I was afraid to strike them. They were only children and I didn't want to hurt them. By the time I understood the seriousness of my trouble, there was no way for me to fight so many who were so small, so fast, and so fearless. I'd toss one off only to have five more leap at my back. They were like monkeys, clinging to my clothes, making sounds that weren't words.

"I crumpled beneath them. They robbed me; I had

only five hundred pesos, but I suppose that was a great deal to them. They jabbed me with their sticks and swatted me with their thin little switches that stung like whips. I covered my head with my arms. A dozen pairs of tiny hands slid in and out of my pockets, down my pants, inside my shoes." He stood up and shook himself as if those hands were moving inside his clothes now. He walked over to the girl and looked down at her.

"I thought they would kill me. I thought they would go on pounding and beating me until I was unconscious, that in their inexperience they wouldn't know when to quit and I would be smothered, my nose and mouth ground into the dirt."

He turned and paced, slapping the air with his hands as he gestured toward the mantel. "But I was lucky, you see. A remarkable thing happened: they jumped off me, scattered, and disappeared before I had time to lift my head and wipe the dust out of my eyes; I had been spared, miraculously, I thought. I was almost a convert—until I saw the lights of a police jeep patrolling the area. In my ignorance, I flagged them down, thinking they would round up the little hoodlums within the hour, and the monsters would be punished.

"The two men spoke no English and I couldn't make them understand my Spanish. They dragged me into the jeep. I was kicking and arguing, ready for a fight with someone. If we left, I knew the children would never be caught. One of the men finally twisted my arm behind my back and the other dangled a pair of handcuffs in my face. They didn't need to speak my language to get the message across: I was about to become the criminal rather than the victim, and if I had any sense at all I should go quietly. I did.

"Four hours later they managed to find an official who spoke English. Oh, he was very courteous. He said the police were seriously concerned with the problem of these unruly bands of children. If I would press charges, I would be a great help to them. Most of the foreigners who were attacked wanted to forget the entire incident. Did I think I could identify them? Their faces were a blur, like faces seen from a spinning merry-go-round. Their mouths were open, laughing, yelling. I saw the official smirk. 'Yes, they all look alike, these children; I understand,' he said. I wanted to say no, of course they don't all look alike, but the horrible truth was they did. God, to me they did.

"I thanked him for his help and turned to go. 'Just one more moment of your time, Mr. Brandon, please,' he said. 'I am still wondering, that is a bad part of town, and I would very much like to know what business you had there.' I told him it was not business at all, that I was strictly a tourist in Bogotá, a curious visitor, and I was out exploring. 'May I suggest,' he said, 'that you restrict your explorations to daylight hours and that you stay away from our west side altogether.' I said I appreciated his advice and would most certainly heed it.

"Two days later I got a flight back to New York, and the day after that I drove to Connecticut to see my wife—my ex-wife. I knew she wouldn't be thrilled to have me arrive unannounced, but I was too shaken up to call and fabricate an excuse to visit.

"Anne was logical; that had always been a comfort to me. She could put things in order. I would tell her some version of my story that made me innocent, but not stupid. The children would be older and my life would be at stake."

He faced the girl again, rooting himself three feet from her chair. She was sitting on her hands. Her lips were parted and dry. Her eyes were dry too, from not blinking.

"The second she opened the door I could tell things weren't going to go my way. 'Oh, hello,' she said, 'it's you.' I knew I wouldn't be able to tell her anything. She called to Stephanie. My daughter adored me. I was her glamorous father who swept her off to New York for an intimate dinner twice a month and brought her home asleep.

"She came bounding down the stairs. She leaped at me, her dark hair flying. I jerked away. It was only a reflex, but it took me half a minute too long to recover. My life was altered in thirty seconds. Think about that. Count it out.

"She was fragile, I guess, the divorce and all, the fights she'd overheard. She let out one sob, one inconsolable yelp, and she was back up the stairs before I could say her name. 'Jesus, Ted,' Anne hissed. 'What's wrong with you?' It wasn't a question: it was an accusation. I wanted to tell her—I almost wanted to tell her the truth, minus one or two small details. Anne would say I'd done the right thing, not fighting the children. She would ridicule the smug official, and I would suggest he was on the take, that the kids cut him in to keep him off their backs. Everything would be all right again if Anne would only say it.

"I said, 'I'm sorry. Tell Stephanie I'm sorry. I've been working too hard. I'm not myself.'

"I could almost hear her thoughts: 'Selfish bastard. He'll never change. Even now when he has to give so little, nothing to me, a day every couple of weeks to Stephanie, he still can't think of anyone except himself. Thank god. Thank god I don't love him anymore.' I knew that woman. I really did. And I know enough about you," he said to the girl, "to know you're wondering—"

"—why you didn't follow your daughter upstairs and talk to her," she said.

"And make it right? Because," he said, "I didn't know how. What would I say? 'You scared me, baby'? Do you think that would have been better? Do you think a ten-year-old girl would understand how her father could be afraid of her? And anyway, that's the kind of man I am. Events don't change us. They reveal us to ourselves. Bogotá didn't change me. It exposed me."

She looked down at his feet. Perhaps she understood, perhaps not. It made little difference. Confessions are not made for the one who hears them.

"When I returned to the life in my little attic in Greenwich Village, the poems came, just as I had wished, but at a cost I'd never imagined. Stephanie visited once in the five years I stayed there. I had certain rights, of course, but how could I impose them on her? How could I force her to stay in that hot, cramped place with its low ceilings and tiny windows when she lived on a sprawling acre in Connecticut? It was my prison, not hers.

"I didn't release myself until the night I had a bit too much after a lecture in Boston and passed out at the wheel before I got to New York." He flicked on the light near the girl. "That's how I did this." He leaned over and braced his hands on the arms of the chair, turning his right cheek toward her so she could get a good look at the raw skin that never healed. She took in one gasp of air, then seemed to stop breathing. He was close enough to see her nostrils flare wide. He stood up, unbuttoning his shirt as fast as he could, ripping it open so she could see his scarred, hairless chest. "And this," he said.

She flinched, but looked at it, clenching her teeth as if she were fighting something. Were there tears? He wondered. Pity or fear? Why had he told her what he had told no one else? To have her? There was no chance of that now: he knew he had gone too far and that she'd flee as soon as he gave her the chance. No, to finish it off, he thought, to be done with it, to kill off the last urge to change the past and say: "This is how it will always be." He had chosen her as he had chosen almost every woman in his life, as he had chosen Anne, because she happened to be there at the moment he was ready, because she was willing to hear it, more or less. But it hadn't worked. Nothing had changed. It was like the car spinning in his dreams, the glass burning his skin night after night till he woke beating the cool sheets with his hands. He was desperate to touch her, now that she knew. He lunged, grabbing her breast, lifting her, pressing her against his naked chest, against the small knots of his scars, kissing her nose instead of her mouth.

He expected a struggle, so he gripped her tightly, pinning her arms to her sides. The color was gone from her face. Wispy blond hairs had worked themselves loose from her neat ponytail, and the girl looked much younger than she had at lunch when things were so nicely under control. When he stooped to kiss her this time, he was sure she'd turn her face; and he was ready for that, but instead she stood on her tiptoes, closed her eyes, and opened her mouth enough for his tongue to slip easily between her parted lips.

Yes, at last, the taste of a woman—he had not forgotten. Her legs went slightly limp and she tugged at him as if she wanted to pull him to the floor. Like a throbbing at the back of his head, he heard the words. *Yo me lo piso.* He stood firm. Her thin arms were around his waist and her small hands moved lightly in circles on his back. When he kissed her, he felt towering and huge: he engulfed her. She tried to lead him down again, but it was only a suggestion, really, because he was so much stronger. *Yo me lo piso,* echoed deep in his mind. He didn't want her on the floor. She held her little face turned upward, ready to be kissed, and started unbuttoning her blouse. He put out his hand to cover her neck. "Ted," she said, "it's all right." The words shocked him, as if she had uttered the most vile obscenity, and he almost slapped her.

He gripped her arms and shoved her away from him, backing up until his hands were pressed against the wall. "Get out of here," he said.

She stepped toward him. "I want to," she said.

"You want to what?" he said. "Do an old man a favor? Spare me. There's nothing you can do for me."

He hoped she wouldn't cry. He was in no mood to soothe a weeping girl. In a way, he felt sorry for her, seeing her humiliation, her confusion; but he could offer no solace, and he disliked her even more for this wave of guilt. He wanted to be alone.

To his relief, she proved to be a dignified girl once again. She straightened her shoulders and nodded, unable to form the civil words of departure.

Down the long flights of stairs, her footsteps made a hollow sound. He walked to his front window and watched her splash through the puddles to cross the street. She pulled her skirt above her knees to get away faster. Her legs were strong and muscular. He was an idiot, he thought, to be so rude. Things had gotten out of hand for a minute, that was all. He wanted to call her, persuade her to walk back up his stairs so he could at

least call her a cab and be a gentleman about the whole
thing. The window was jammed. He put his full force
into it, but it wouldn't budge and he could see it had
been painted shut. He thought of slamming his fist
through the pane; but the girl was a block away, and
thinking about breaking glass with his own hand kept
him from doing it. Young men did things like that on
impulse, but he was not young. He had enough scars.
Someone mad with love might destroy a window to call
to a girl, but he was a long way from that.

He stood with his palms flattened against the glass.
The rain had washed the window almost clean. He wondered if the girl with the strong thighs could have been
some comfort, but as he put his lips to the glass it was
Anne's name he whispered, "Anne, Anne." Even now,
after all these years, he had told the story only for her, to
unwind the years, run backward to that day, to explain
and weep and be forgiven, to stop Stephanie before she
darted up the stairs and before his life was made irrevo-
cably separate from their lives, from every other life.
Anne was right. He was selfish in those days, as only a
handsome man can be when he is vain enough to think he
will always find some woman willing to shelter him. Yes,
at times he was as selfish as a screaming infant who thinks
the whole world is there just waiting to answer his cry;
but he wished her to know, oh god more than anything
in this hour, that he was not, not nearly, as selfish as she
thought.

Lizards

CAL LIFTED THE ROCK and Dora snatched the lizard. She was quicker than her brother even though he had stopped wearing the maroon bathrobe. Now he could run and squat. His legs weren't tangled in heavy woolen cloth and his back didn't itch with sweat under the blaze of the Arizona sun. And he had learned to grip the lizards right around the belly, the way Dora did, because if you pinched one by the tail, it fell off and the misshapen creature scuttled out of reach.

Cal had told Dora not to worry about the tails; they'd grow back. But now Dora informed him that the tail *regenerated*. She liked the word and said it twice because she was eight and Cal was twelve, and she was proud of all the things she knew that he didn't. She also told him, *for his information*, that his former clumsiness was cruel, and that if he didn't catch the lizards fairly, the way she did, then he shouldn't catch them at all. Yes, the tails regenerated, but the new tails were never quite as good as the old ones: they were too short or too narrow, shriveled at the end or crooked at the base of the spine. The lizards would never be as fast, their balance never as perfect. If they became easy prey, Cal was to blame.

Usually Dora kept the lizards in a shoe box only for a few hours. She liked to open the lid just a crack to peek at their glassy eyes in the dark, liked to tell them she could keep them there as long as she wanted. But after she told them that, she always turned the box on its side and let them go free in the grass.

Cal wouldn't let her dump them this time. He said he wanted to keep them until after lunch, and she agreed: he was still the oldest.

After they ate their ham sandwiches, after Dora ate Cal's ham and he ate her bread, Dora realized Cal had tricked her. The box was not behind the couch where they had stuffed it when they came inside. Dora told her big sister and Allison told their mother. Mom whispered a nasty word under her breath before she asked him what he'd done with the lizards.

"I let them go."

"Then where's the box?" said Dora. She had him now.

"I threw it out back in the dumpster. They messed it."

"Liar!" Allison said.

Cal peered at his bare toes. First one wiggled and then another; they amused him.

"Three of them were mine," Dora said. "I caught them. They were mine to let go."

"They stank," said Cal.

Cal's mother didn't look as if she believed him, but what could she do? She told all three of the children they could go swimming at two if they stayed out of her hair till then. It was half past noon.

Cal knew what his mother would do as soon as she was alone, knew she would draw all the shades to block the afternoon sun before she ran a cool bath. He imagined her lying in the tub, her stomach swelling above the water like the curved back of some rare white whale. It was late August. The baby was due at the end of September, but his mother had looked ready to bust since June.

Cal thought of his mother soaking in the tepid water, smoking her long cigarettes, one after another, here, sunk down low in the tub, the only place she could be by herself. When Cal's father came home, he'd sniff the air and say "What's that smell?" just so Cal's mother would remember she had no secrets.

Cal watched the three Scofield boys romp by the pool. They didn't have to wait to go swimming. Their mother didn't have to sit on the steps in the shade, waiting— almost expecting—one of them to panic. Cal wondered

what his mother would do if he floundered, swallowed
water and flapped at the surface with useless flipper
hands. Surely she would not plunge into the pool. He
imagined her trying to dive to the bottom as he sank. He
would drop away from her, heavy as a bag of rocks, and
she would bob back to the surface, her bloated middle
keeping her ridiculously afloat.

Still, they had to wait. Perhaps she thought the children would be safe if she watched them, that nothing
could happen as long as she was sitting on the cement
steps. *God is watching you,* he remembered Reverend
Sykes saying the last time they went to church, just
before they left Montana. *God's eyes keep you safe. Beware
the man who forgets to thank his Lord for this protection. Beware the man who by indifference dares the Lord to look away.*

The biggest Scofield brother ran the length of the
diving board, bounced and started spinning. His powerful legs made the board shudder. He hit the water with
a splat that must have stung his chest, but he came up
grinning.

Cal didn't like the Scofields. He knew that when he
started junior high in another week the two oldest ones
would walk behind him, charging toward his back to tug
his book bag, or step on his heels, whistling nonchalantly
if he were fool enough to turn around. Allison would be
in sixth grade. She'd hold Dora's hand as they walked in
the opposite direction, toward the elementary school, so
she wouldn't be there to put her fists on her hips and tell
the boys to get lost. The youngest one was harmless

when he was alone. He might follow Cal's sisters, but he wouldn't dare speak to the girls, or touch them.

The three brothers were stocky as little men. A fuzz of blond hair covered their legs. As they stretched in the sun or wrestled in the grass, Cal was ashamed to watch. Their wet swimming suits clung to their muscled bottoms like second skins, scarlet and translucent.

Just after midnight, her mother and father found Allison in the living room, trying to scale the wall. She had one foot on the window frame and the other on the back of a chair. Pressing her body flat to the wall, she slithered as if she thought she were making steady progress, though in fact she could climb no higher. Her parents stood in the dark, silent, afraid to startle her, afraid that if she woke she'd fall.

She hadn't walked in her sleep for years. As a small child in Montana, she had paced the hallway at night, hiked up and down the stairs, opened every door of the house. But in the Arizona apartment, the only place to go was up the wall.

"What the hell?" her father said, forgetting to whisper.

"Shush, you'll wake her."

"What's she doing?"

"Climbing the wall," said Allison's mother.

"I see that."

"She thinks she's a lizard."

"How do you know?"

"Look at her."

They did look at their daughter. She wore only a T-shirt and underwear. Allison was thin and light-boned, fragile at the wrists and ankles, a breakable child. She dug her fingernails into the stucco and lifted her legs one at a time, knees bent, thighs rubbing the rough plaster.

"What should we do?" said her father.

"Wait. All we can do is wait for her to get tired."

"Shit."

"*You* don't have to. You go back to bed."

"Sure you don't mind?"

"I was restless anyway."

"I've got a meeting in the morning."

"I said I don't mind."

"Otherwise I'd keep you company."

"Go to bed, Stan."

He pecked her cheek and shuffled down the hall. She watched him; he was a tall man with narrow shoulders. His arms seemed too long and his pajamas hung off his flat bottom.

Allison's mother lowered herself onto the couch. There was no such thing as simply sitting down or standing up anymore; every movement involved careful calculation, a subtle shift of weight, one arm braced, legs solidly planted.

Allison seemed to be slowing down. Maybe she thought she was near the top. But the top of what? Not just a wall—a sand dune, the slick rock face of a cliff. Yes, that would be an accomplishment.

Allison's mother didn't mind sitting up, watching. It was nice to be the only one awake, to have this time alone in the dark. She remembered when the night journeys began. Allison was still a baby, and her mother would find her climbing over the side of the crib and then climbing back, all the time saying: "In, out. In, out . . ." No wonder she was famished by morning and woke wailing. But Allison did not risk climbing out of the crib when she was awake. No, she pulled herself up by the bars and stood, a little prisoner, furiously rattling her cage, her face blotched and red. Her mother couldn't get to her fast enough. By the time the bottle was ready, Allison's whole body trembled, and as she drank the tears continued to roll down her cheeks.

But no matter how hungry she was, she never took more than half a bottle. She had a small stomach. So Cal waited, patiently, beside her crib. When Allison had had all she wanted, she passed the bottle through the bars for him to finish. Even then he depended on her.

At last Allison climbed down from the chair. Her eyes were open but blind, and she stood in the middle of the living room as if she didn't know where to go now that she was no longer a lizard on the wall. Her mother took her hand and led her back to bed.

In the morning, the inside of Allison's thighs were raw from chafing against the stucco wall. Mystified, she showed her mother the sore skin.

"Must be a rash," her mother said. She was afraid to tell Allison what she'd done in the night. Children could be shocked by their own secrets. A grown man would not be surprised to learn he drank too much gin and danced barefoot across the neighbor's lawn. The next day, he'd sit still and let his wife pluck the prickers from the soles of his feet. But children cannot bear such humiliations. Allison would not want to envision herself pressed to the wall, realizing that her own father had seen her wearing nothing but her underpants and a T-shirt.

Still, some knowledge of the night's obsessions lingered. She had lizards on her mind. At breakfast she said Cal had probably hidden them somewhere that they couldn't get any air. That would be just like him. "Stupid," she said. They'd rot. They'd stink. The whole apartment would reek of dead lizard. He swore he had already let them go. "Yesterday," he said, and Dora kicked him under the table.

But the lizards weren't free. They were still in the box in the hall closet, crawling on top of one another's scaly backs. That's where Cal's mother found them later that morning when she was looking for clean towels to hang in the bathroom.

Her yell brought all three children running. "I knew it," Allison said. Dora seized the box and darted outside. No one stopped her. She was going to be the one to let the lizards go after all. Cal stood still for his scolding, and Allison stayed to watch.

His mother told him he was never to bring those

awful things in the apartment again. "I don't know what I'll do," she said, "if I ever find another lizard in this house."

Cal hated threats like that. He wished she would be more specific so he could imagine a whack on the butt or four days without pool privileges. *I don't know what I'll do* sounded dangerous. She might lock herself in the bathroom for half the day. She might scream herself hoarse. She might pack her overnight bag, the way she did that time in Montana. Only this time she might really go.

Cal's mother knew he didn't want to go back to school. She was ready to bribe and bargain, ready to scare him with tales of the wasted lives of boys who neglected their educations, boys with no futures who pumped gas or delivered newspapers, who robbed grocery stores and went to jail, all those boys who could have been anything—if they'd only stayed in school.

Last year he'd missed six weeks, and he'd worn that damn wool robe every day. He slogged through the apartment, stiff as an old man. He held his hands over his ears when his sisters talked too loudly at the dinner table. And even Cal's mother was surprised when she took him to the doctor and saw her son sitting there on the edge of the examining table wearing nothing but his socks and shorts. All this time she had berated him for wearing that filthy robe, and now she realized there was something wrong: a hidden cancer, an insidious parasite. She saw each bone of his chest, his knobby elbows, his sharp ribs. Under the harsh light, his skin was so pale it seemed almost blue. She kept staring at his ears because it was alarming to see such large ears on a skinny child. They were healthy and pink, surprisingly fleshy. She covered her mouth, but her eyes revealed everything. Cal nodded, suddenly wise beyond his years.

But there was no disease. The doctor said Cal looked like a child who was recovering slowly from some grave illness, as if he had survived meningitis, or lain in a coma for months after a car accident. Now he was moving, step by step, back into the world of the living.

He had gained five pounds over the summer and had stopped wearing the robe. But the whole thing might start again. Cal's mother could measure out her life by her children's illnesses: there were the mumps in '57 and the measles in '59. Everything came in threes—was passed from one child to the next. Each disease lingered in their house for a month or more; a common flu was a menace. In 1960 the flood brought a typhoid scare and the shots made them all weak and nauseated. They lay sprawled in the living room, the whole family, curled in chairs or stretched out on the floor, clutching blankets, dreading the real fever. She was sick from the shots too; her arm ached. Still she fetched juice and made tea for Stan and the children.

Yes, it could start so easily. And the disease a boy invents may be worse than the illness he endures.

Cal stared at the maroon bathrobe hanging in the closet. He longed to put it on, to feel the scratchy wool on his neck, the tiresome weight. The robe made his body unimportant, made him stop thinking about himself. The bristly warmth reminded him that God was watching. *Beware the man who by indifference dares the Lord to look away.* The robe protected him, saved him from his own forgetfulness.

He remembered his mother's threat: last year she told his father she was at the end of her rope. She thought they should consider a military school for Cal, somewhere with rules he'd have to follow, a regular routine and plenty of exercise. Cal thought a military camp on the desert outside Flagstaff sounded worse than any junior high in Scottsdale. But he didn't see why he had to go to junior high at all. There was still plenty to learn in sixth grade. He'd missed the last month and a half of school. Even with his mother's tutoring, he'd barely passed the final exams in math and grammar. He could do the whole year again and wait for Allison.

If he were back home in Montana, he knew what he'd do. He'd hide in the cellar. He'd dig a cave for himself in the earth wall and curl up in the damp, cool dirt till he fell asleep. They'd call and call. Dad would be at work, but his mother and his sisters would open every closet door, poke their heads under every bed, run outside and shout his name down the alley and the street. But he wouldn't hear; no, he wouldn't want to hear. And if they found him it would be too late to send him to school. His mother would have to take a brush to his back and scalp. Later, he'd watch her pick the worms off his clothes.

There were dozens of places to hide in Montana: in the wood box, underneath the bathroom sink, in the cluttered garage—he could miss school for weeks. But there was nowhere to hide in this apartment. He shared his bedroom with his sisters, with only the five-foot-high bookcase between their beds. The closet was his refuge, but they all knew just where to find him.

He wondered where the baby was going to sleep. It didn't matter. No wall was thick enough to muffle squalls in the night, no corner deep enough to keep him safe from the desperate sound of hunger cries.

Cal was right about the new school. He didn't like it. And he was right about the Scofield brothers: they did run up behind him to step on his heels. He didn't turn around, didn't jab the air with his fists, or make a fool of himself yelling till his voice cracked. He gave them no satisfaction at all except for the misery of his flushed neck.

He did like Miss Faye, Miss Louise Faye. She had straight blond hair cut off blunt at the shoulders; she wasn't too tall. She moved with a clipped, hard stride, and she didn't mess around with silly introductions or make them stand up one at a time to say something memorable about their summer vacations. She got right to business, to their first math problem. She wrote it on the board quickly. Her numbers were big; her lines wide and confident. The chalk made ticking sounds as it hit the slate.

Cal didn't know what to do, but the others were all opening their notebooks, scribbling out figures, adding 6 and 9, subtracting 2, then multiplying by 8. They went much too fast for Cal; Miss Faye was already writing the second problem, but he kept scribbling. The fat, tanned boy beside him had the first answer: 104. He shouted it out. Miss Faye laughed and said, "That's right," then asked him, very politely, Cal thought, not to say the answers till everyone had a chance to finish. Cal had only made it to 13.

After school, Miss Faye asked to see Cal's notes for the day. She said she knew he'd missed a lot of school last year and she wanted to be sure he wasn't behind. She could have said it in a mean way to make him feel stupid and slow, but she didn't: she said it in a voice that made him think the numbers on his page mattered to her.

She sat down beside him and showed him three different ways to multiply 13 by 8. Her fingernails were clean, her fingers short and thick. He liked the last one best: $(10 \times 8) + (3 \times 8)$. No teacher had ever told him there was more than one way to multiply. No one had ever said, as Miss Faye did, that he should use the technique that was easiest for him, that no single method was right or better than any other, that different people use different routes to get the same answer.

Even Mrs. Grossman in Montana, who was kind and old and very patient, thought there was only one way to multiply. Cal wanted to write Mrs. Grossman a letter and show her all the paths that led to the right answer. But he knew it would hurt her feelings if he said how smart Miss Faye was, how fast she worked, how good she smelled when she sat beside him, a lemon-soap smell, not the sticky perfume of damp talc. No, he wouldn't tell anyone about clever Miss Faye.

When his mother scuffed through the kitchen, her thongs slapping the linoleum, her back arched with the weight of her belly, he wouldn't tell her how Miss Faye skipped from one side of the chalkboard to the other, writing math problems joyfully, as if the numbers revealed some secret delight.

When Cal's father made him remake his bed to get the corners right, Cal wouldn't announce there were different ways to do things, three ways to multiply. Night after night, when Mother told Dora the proper way to set a table, he wouldn't say: *Let her do it her own way.*

Miss Faye gave him a whole page of math problems, "Not an assignment," she explained, "just to practice when you feel like it, maybe one or two a night. Write out every step, and show me when you're finished."

Cal couldn't wait to get home and shut himself in his closet. He barely noticed the Scofield brothers cavorting by the pool. The one who was in his class yelled, "Hey Monkey Ears, did teacher keep you after school already?" For once he didn't care. He trotted past the boys, smiling, squeezing his notebook and the precious math problems to his chest. As he skipped inside the house, a Scofield shouted, "Hey, you deaf?" And another Scofield said, "Can't be deaf with ears like that."

Cal stayed in his closet till dinner and did six problems. As soon as he was excused from the table, he got back to work. He did all twenty. It was slow at first, but it was quicker when he saw the patterns, and by the end he was doing each one three different ways, writing out each step, just the way Miss Faye told him.

In the morning, he was too excited to eat breakfast and his cornflakes got soggy in the milk.

"Don't think you can play sick and stay home with me all day," his mother said.

Cal shook his head but didn't explain that he *wanted* to go to school and that's why he couldn't eat his cereal. He heard the way his mother said *stay home with me,* and even though she wouldn't let him, he sensed she would not like to know how anxious he was to see Miss Faye.

He thought he remembered his mother was pretty, with soft, pale skin, but now her forehead and arms were splotched with dry patches, itchy sores that she picked until they bled. Her cheeks had grown puffy, so fat that her nose and eyes seemed much too small. Cal stared. "What is it?" his mother said. He grabbed his books and ran out the door.

Miss Faye wore knee socks and loafers, a dark blue skirt with dozens of pleats that twirled as she turned from the board to the class and back again. Cal kept the unbearable secret all day. It was too valuable to spill, too important to waste when there wasn't time enough to enjoy her praise. He knew she probably thought he hadn't done a single problem. He knew she was too kind to ask.

After school, after everyone else had dashed for the door, Cal approached her desk and laid the notebook in front of her, an offering, a gift. She turned the pages slowly, smiling, nodding. "Perfect," she said, touching his arm lightly, "every single one is perfect."

He was Lord of the Numbers. Each night Miss Faye gave him a new page of problems, much harder than any of the other kids could do. She showed him how to use decimals and how to find square roots on a slide rule. Sometimes she ruffled his hair when he showed her his work. Once she hugged him: his cheek touched her cheek; her hair brushed against his face. For a long time afterward he felt the pressure of her hands on his back.

He could control numbers, play with them, make them do whatever he wanted. There was only one answer, but there were so many ways to find it. When he tried to read, the words leaped all over the page. Stories never meant what he thought they did. When Miss Faye had other students read their book reports, Cal always

wondered if they had read the same book. Maybe someone was playing a joke on him and giving him a different
story with the same title. Of course he knew that wasn't
true because all the characters had the same names. But
why did everyone else think Robinson Crusoe and his
man Friday were such fine companions when Cal thought
Crusoe was selfish, treating Friday like a friend one day
and a servant the next? These things confused him, so
Cal went back to his numbers.

On the third Monday, Miss Faye was not at her desk. A
much older woman with a high, squeaky voice sat in her
place. "Miss Faye is sick today," she said. And Cal let
out his breath. Just one day. He could last one day. The
big lady with the wrinkled neck told the class her name,
but Cal had forgotten it by the time he got home.

He tried to work on his math in the closet, but he
couldn't concentrate. He ran all the way to school the
next morning. It was too early to go inside. He pulled
himself up on the ledge to look in the window, hoping to
catch a glimpse of Miss Faye: everything would be all
right if he could just see her. But the old woman was still
at the desk. She dozed, leaning back in the chair, her
mouth open, her lips slack. Cal imagined her wheezy
breath and the whiny sound of her voice, the voice that
said, "Now, children—quiet."

During the math lesson, Mrs. Milliken paced the
room. Today she had written her name on the board,
and Cal had copied it in his notebook so that he would

remember. She said she'd be with them till the end of the week—at least—but she still didn't say what was wrong with Miss Faye. She hovered over Cal and watched him work the third problem. He heard her clear her throat like an old man about to spit, but he didn't look up; he stayed hunched over his paper, his eyes so close to the page he could barely see. Finally, she snatched the paper away from him and held it up to the light. She pinched the page between two fingers just at the top corner, as if the paper were a filthy thing.

"What's this?" she squeaked. Her high voice was a drill aimed at his ear. He couldn't answer. He didn't know what she meant. But Mrs. Milliken expected no reply. "You've done the same problem three times." The other students turned to stare. The little girls tittered, hiding their lips with their hands. "Waste of time," the voice whined. "The best way, the fastest way." Cal's face was huge and red, a bright balloon full of hot gas. The voice droned on. "How, may I ask, do you ever expect to finish?" The faces lurched in and out of focus, mouths open, laughing, laughing, but his balloon face didn't burst and the laughter had no sound. Mrs. Milliken gave the paper back to him. "It's dangerous to have too many options," she said. "You're bound to get things wrong."

Dangerous knowledge, Reverend Sykes was always talking about that back in Montana. He said man was better off in the garden before he had any choices. Yes, that was man's burden ever since that fool Eve ate the apple and came to know more than a woman was ever meant to know. Now man had options. He had to make decisions. Oh, and there were so many forks along the road of righteousness, so many paths that started out clear and ended in a dark tangle of thorns and brambles.

The price of wisdom was dear. The serpent became the most cursed of all creatures, despised and feared, told he would go upon his belly and eat dust. The snake was less than a lizard, Cal thought. The lizard got to keep its stubby legs. Eve was punished too. God multiplied her pain in childbearing, yet he made her desire her husband. And God told Eve her husband would rule over her. Adam also tasted the fruit, so God cast both man and woman from the garden. He was afraid they might eat from the tree of life as they had eaten from the tree of knowledge. They would live forever as little gods; they might dare to challenge him.

But did Adam's misery match Eve's? Cal wondered. The earth beyond the garden was hard and dry. Adam and his sons labored all the days of their lives. Still, this didn't seem so bad. Cal had asked his father about Adam's punishment. "Did he have to suffer too?" said Cal.

Cal's father stroked his chin; his glasses slid down his nose, and he peered over them. He looked like a thoughtful man. "Oh my, yes," he said, "Adam suffered—he had to put up with Eve bitching about her pain. And not just in childbearing—if you get my meaning."

Cal didn't "get his meaning" but he knew that listening to someone complain wasn't nearly as bad as scraping your own knee or bumping your own head. Adam got off easy, no matter what his father said.

Now Cal worried about his mother's pain. The baby was due in less than a week. He realized that he had hurt her too, just by being born. He thought that mothers must always hate their children in a way, the way he hated the Scofield brothers when one stuck his foot in his path and the other shoved him from behind. But the sting of a bloody knee was nothing compared with the agony of God's wrath.

Cal did the problems the way Mrs. Milliken said, but he was no longer the Lord of the Numbers, and when he got his paper back the next day, half the problems were marked with a red *x*.

When Miss Faye didn't return the following Monday, the rumors started. Mark Scofield, the brother in Cal's class, said she had probably got herself knocked up and had gone somewhere "to take care of it." Luke Scofield, who was a year older, said she was knocked up for sure, and the father was some stocky Mexican she'd met on vacation. But she wasn't going "to take care of it"; she'd gone to Mexico to live in an airless shack with the dark-skinned man and their little brown baby.

Some of the girls insisted that the father was a blond actor and that Miss Faye had eloped. The child would be blond like its parents, and after it was born, she would send the class a picture of the three of them with a note that said she was very sorry for leaving, but they were all very happy and living in Hollywood. "PS," she'd write, "Hank"—that was her husband's name—"is going to be in a movie with Frank Sinatra. Imagine!" And the girls did imagine. Breathless with giggles, they thought of the actors they wanted to marry.

A few of the less romantic children said the father was a married man, and that Miss Faye had gone to a home for single mothers to have her child in secret and give it away without ever holding it in her arms.

Cal sat in his closet, hugging his knees. The numbers blurred on the page. He had forgotten the multiplication tables overnight. There were three options and they all made him miserable. He didn't want to think of Miss Faye being pregnant, didn't want her ankles to swell or her hair to turn brittle. She wouldn't have the patience to explain long division; and if she sat beside him, she wouldn't smell like herself.

His parents were whispering about Miss Faye when he came into the kitchen before dinner, but they hushed as soon as they saw him. They must have heard the rumors too, and they'd think she was a bad woman. He knew the blond actor was the lesser of three evils, that's what his mother would say, but Cal didn't think it made much difference. No matter who the father was, Miss Faye had deserted him.

Somewhere, she sat in a dark room, the windows closed, the shades drawn. When Cal thought of her, he saw her belly swelling by the minute, as if she were being pumped full of air. Her thighs spread, her wrists grew thick—even her face stretched. She began to laugh in a frightening way, a low, bottomless chortle. She was twice her normal size and still expanding. She was too big to fit through the door. Soon she was half the size of the room. Cal screwed his eyes shut and rubbed them with his knuckles to make her go away.

Dora got out of school a half hour earlier than Allison, so her mother had to walk the five blocks in the blistering heat of midafternoon. It took her nearly a half hour. Often she had to stop to lean up against a building in the thin line of shade. Every day she wondered if this would be the day she didn't make it. Every day she thought: *What if it starts—right here?*

Today was worse than usual. It was so hot the sky was bleached white, burned dry. The air scratched her throat and felt like dust in her lungs. There was nothing in the house for dinner. Dora's mother thought of calling Stan to stop for something on the way home from work, but she couldn't bear the thought of the tone of voice he'd use with her. She could have the kids all ready to go to Nick's Burger Delight when Stan got home, but she'd done that three times this month. Stan would complain about the size of his burger, and Allison would fuss about the pickles. At some point during the meal, one of the children would spill a carton of milk and Stan would yell too loudly, making people turn and shake their heads as they counted the children and gauged the size of the mother's stomach. Dora would cry whether she was the one to spill the milk or not.

No, going to Nick's again was not a good idea. It was easier to walk the three extra blocks and buy a chicken from the butcher. But she'd have to talk Dora into it.

Dora could not be bribed or tempted. Neither the promise of an ice-cream soda at Woolworth's nor the offer of a quarter for her bank could induce her to walk to the butcher shop. Her mother had made the mistake of saying, "Can we walk down to the market to get something for dinner?" She thought she was clever, putting it that way, so sweetly, but Dora shook her head with determination, and her mother cursed herself for giving the child a choice. Never *ask* Dora anything, she reminded herself. "We're going to the market," she said.

Dora gazed at something far beyond her mother, a disappearing car, a shimmering mirage of a lake wavering on the hot street. She looked more like a very short adult than an eight-year-old child. Her sturdy limbs revealed no trace of girlish frailty. When she squinted at the sun, the lines at the corners of her eyes were deep and old.

Her mother tried to take her hand, but Dora pulled away.

"I'm coming," she said.

The child lagged. She crouched on the sidewalk to study bugs. While they shopped, she refused to help carry any of the groceries so her mother had to settle for just enough food to get them through one more meal.

Two blocks from home, Dora announced that she wasn't going another step. Watery blood from the chicken leaked through the paper bag, and the sack was beginning to disintegrate.

"Just another two blocks, sweetheart," her mother said.

"I can't." Dora plopped herself down in the shade of a scrubby little tree.

"I have to get this chicken in the fridge, honey."

"I'm too hot."

"I'm hot too, but the apartment's nice and cool."

"I'm not going."

"Are you planning on staying here all night?"

"I'm just resting."

"How long?" her mother said. The bottom of the sack gave way, coming apart in her hands.

"I don't know."

"Mommy has to take the groceries home."

"Okay."

"I can't leave you here."

"Why not?"

How could she explain? *You might run away.* No, Dora wasn't going another step. *Someone might steal you.* She'd warned her children not to talk to strangers, not to take candy or go near cars.

"Don't be a baby, Dora."

Dora glared at her mother's belly. "I'm not a baby," she said, very slowly, one word at a time.

"If I bring your bike, will you ride it home?"

"Maybe."

No promises. Dora was past the point of bargaining. Her mother's hands were sticky with chicken blood.

"You'll stay right here?"

Dora nodded.

"Won't move an inch?"

She nodded again.

"Promise Mommy?"

Dora sighed, as if she found her mother very tiresome or very stupid.

Dora's mother ran, at least she tried to run. She could smell the chicken. Nothing will happen, she told herself. But ever since that incident with Cal's teacher, she was afraid. Violence was random. She could take the red wagon and pull Dora home. No, she was already exhausted. The bike was easier. She wondered if she should tell Cal the truth about Miss Faye. She guessed what the kids had been saying. She believed in being honest with children, but Stan said no, this was one time when the rumors would do less harm than the truth.

Dora's mother didn't bother to unwrap the chicken. She dropped it in a pan and slid it into the refrigerator along with the lettuce and tomatoes. She wanted to wash her hands and face but didn't dare to waste the time. As she wheeled Dora's bike down the sidewalk, she wished she could ride it, but she was afraid of toppling over on her stomach, a hilarious sight. Her water would break for sure, and there she'd be: a fat lady sitting in her own puddle.

Dora was asleep. Her mother didn't wake her for a moment. She stood, watching the peaceful girl, enjoying those few seconds when she could admire Dora's plump legs and rosy mouth.

The child woke, grumpy and confused. She seemed surprised to find herself outside. She refused to talk or ride the bike, so her mother had to wheel it home with one hand and drag Dora along with the other.

Dora's mother couldn't get cool. Her dress stuck to her sweaty back. It was too late to take a bath and not worth the trouble to change her clothes. Cal and Allison had come home already, dropped their shoes by the door and disappeared. Dora revived and went out to find her brother and sister. Soon their mother would have to start dinner. She was just going to lie down on the couch for a minute, just until her legs stopped throbbing, until the blood stopped banging against her temples. She draped a wet rag over her face.

That's how Stan found her an hour and a half later. He looked at her and walked into the kitchen. There was a loaf of bread on the table but nothing on the stove. He opened the fridge and saw the chicken, still wrapped in the torn white paper, sitting in a pool of pink water. He ambled back to the living room to stare at his wife. Her breathing was deep and even. The cloth covered her face. He thought she was asleep, so he jiggled the keys in his pocket.

"Not a word," she said. "Not one damn word."

The children wandered in from outside. When Allison saw her mother, she pulled a chair toward the cupboard and climbed up to reach the Cheerios and the Sugar Frosted Flakes. Cal got the milk and Dora turned on the fan. Their father stood in the doorway watching them.

Cal imagined Miss Faye across the border, living with her Mexican lover in that shack with a dirt floor. He thought this story was the most believable; he told himself the man had kidnapped Miss Faye when he found out about the baby. She was biding her time till it was born. She had grown brown as a Mexican herself, but her hair was still shiny blond. She'd be easy to find. Cal meant to track her. He'd help her trick that Mexican, that short man with the thick thighs. Cal saw himself and Miss Faye running, saw their black silhouettes against the deep blue of the night sky. Wild dogs barked in the hills. The perfume of flowering cacti made him dizzy, and the desert wind spun the stars into a whirlpool of light. Miss Faye had to rest often, but he understood. He pushed her damp hair behind her ears and poured water from his canteen onto her feet.

At the playground behind the apartment building, Cal looked for lizards. He wanted to catch a dozen or more. He would let them go in the Mexican's house, and the big-armed bully would be so busy chasing them out the door with a broom that he wouldn't notice Miss Faye was gone.

Cal had no box, only his empty book bag. His luck

was bad. For a half hour or more he didn't even see a lizard. Finally he spotted one miserable creature under the teeter-totter. The pitiful runt had a crooked tail, and he wondered if this was one he'd caught before, one whose tail he'd destroyed before he learned to grasp the belly.

He pursued it ruthlessly and clenched it much too hard. The tiny monster twisted in his fist, scratching at his fingers, opening its mouth in a silent roar. He held it tight as he stuffed it deep into the dark bag. The rubbery underside of the animal gave him a sick feeling in his stomach, and he heard his mother say, *I don't know what I'll do if you ever bring those filthy things in this house again.* He wondered if he should forget the whole plan. He could find some other diversion. But how would his mother ever know? There was no reason to worry. He caught three more and headed home. Tomorrow he'd come back to the playground. When he had enough, he'd head for Mexico.

In his closet, Cal dumped his Sunday shoes and put the four lizards in the box. They climbed over one another; their eyes never closed. That night he slid them under his bed and listened to them scratching at the cardboard. They were always moving. He heard Dora's heavy breath beyond the bookcase, heard her sigh in her sleep. He pictured Miss Faye stretched out on a dirty grass mat, tossing back and forth, waiting for him. His mother waddled down the hallway toward the bathroom. His father snored. Cal couldn't hear him but he was sure.

The lizards crawled up the sides of the box. Their tails twitched. Their lidless eyes rolled in the dark. Cal stayed awake and counted the five trips his mother made to the bathroom in the night.

The Scofield brothers had learned the truth about Miss Faye; and by the time Cal got to school, everyone in the schoolyard knew. There was no married man or blond actor, no barrel-chested Mexican. There was no baby. Miss Faye was in the hospital, her face wrapped in bandages.

The Scofield boys acted out the crime again and again: Paul pounced on every yellow-haired girl who passed, holding her close while she kicked and wriggled. He breathed the words in her ear: *Don't forget me, pretty lady*, while his brother Mark drew the startling line with a thick red pen. Cal watched one of the girls struggle. Mark yanked her hair to keep her head still. Her skirt was pulled up exposing her pale thighs. Cal caught a glimpse of her white underpants. She looked him in the eye and knew what he'd seen.

The Scofields got five girls. Two teachers tried to interfere, but Mark slashed the air with his red pen, and the women backed away. Finally, Mr. Wright, the principal, stopped them. He grabbed their shirts at the neck and twisted, one in each hand, as if he meant to choke the boys. An eighth-grade teacher said, "Careful, Marty," and Mr. Wright loosened his grip. He told the Scofields to wait for him in his office. "And don't get any bright ideas about cutting out," he said.

The story emerged in spouts and whispers. What the children didn't know they made up and wove into the truth until facts and fallacies were inseparable. What did it matter? The man who did this to Miss Faye was the kind who *might* have kept a tarantula as a pet.

Miss Faye had met him at a ranch outside Phoenix last summer. She'd gone horseback riding for the day; he worked in the stable but pretended he owned the place. He said he might drive into Scottsdale some evening and she said fine. He said he might call and take her out to dinner if he knew how to find her. He was tall, his face dark, hardened by the desert sun. He talked real slow and made it clear that it didn't matter much either way. Miss Faye gave him her number.

A week later he came to the city. He seemed different in town. Miss Faye noticed his horse-sweat smell and gritty hands. His face was creased and had a mean look even when he smiled. She didn't want to go to dinner, but it was too late for excuses. Sitting high in the cab of his truck, she realized he had more than dirt on his boots. The ripe scent filled the air.

Going out to dinner meant eating a burger and fries at a drive-in joint. *Don't care much for restaurants*, he mumbled. She had to choke down her food, smelling him and the place where he worked the whole time.

Parked in front of her house, he kissed her hard, forced his tongue in her mouth and started pawing at her breasts. He laughed when she pushed him away; he knotted her hair in his fist and kissed her as long as he wanted.

Soon he tired of fighting. He said *Fine*. He said, *So you think you're too good for me? You're nothing special Miss High and Mighty. I don't have a fancy education, but I know a thing or two.*

That's when he pulled his pet tarantula from behind the seat. He kept the hairy creature in a little wooden cage, and he held it right up in her face. The overgrown spider raised its front legs and reared its horrible bulbous head. "Tarantulas hunt by touch," he said. "They can feel the footsteps of a mouse."

Miss Faye fumbled for the door. He didn't try to stop her. No sir, he was enjoying himself too much. A pet like that can come in handy. A pet like that is good company for a man.

The next time he called she was busy. The third time she said she was leaving town for a few days. The fourth time he swore and called her names. The fifth time he just breathed hard and said, "I'm watching you."

She didn't notice his truck parked around the corner that night in the middle of September. She didn't see the tall, lean man lurking in the shadows. Her first clue was the tarantula that charged her feet as she opened the screen door. But that was much too late. He clamped his hand over her mouth and took the knife to her face. *That'll teach you to be so choosy. Don't forget me, pretty lady.* Three seconds—that was all it took. In three seconds, her whole life changed.

All day, the children added to the story until the tale was complete. The marked girls sat in class, wiping at the red lines that wouldn't wash off. Two of them went home, but the mothers of the other three could not be reached, and the girls had to stay, scratching at their cheeks until their skin was rough and sore.

Cal ran the whole way home, but Allison was already in the kitchen, breathlessly telling their mother the version of the story the youngest Scofield had brought to her school.

"And she's going to have this awful scar, five inches long, and they'll have to do plastic surgery, but she'll never look the same."

Cal's mother saw him in the doorway. There wasn't time to explain, wasn't even time to say "Oh, Cal," before he ducked into his room and slammed the door of his closet. She followed him and stood outside, leaning against the wall. His closet door had no lock, but she didn't try the knob.

"Cal?" she said. Her voice was soft, and he imagined her hand on his cheek. He didn't move. "I know you don't believe this right now, but Miss Faye will be all right. It just takes a while for these things to heal."

Cal pounded on the door from the inside and his mother jumped. "Why didn't you tell me?" he yelled.

"I'm sorry, Cal. I was wrong."

His mother had been sorry before, but Cal couldn't remember her ever saying that she was wrong. He didn't answer and he didn't open the door. He listened to his mother breathing; he heard her sigh and go away. The blond girls with the red lines on their faces were with him in the dark. He saw Luke Scofield holding the girl with the bare thighs; he saw her terrified mouth and watched her dig her fingernails into the boy's flesh. Cal felt those fingernails and realized he was clawing at his own arms.

He rubbed his face against his wool bathrobe until it burned. He wanted to wear it again, to sit in the house all day. He heard his mother say: *I'll burn that damn thing.* He heard himself answer: *With me in it?* He knew he could not wear it. He would cut pieces from it and stuff them in his underwear. All day the prickly heat would remind him to think about God. *God's eyes keep you safe,* Reverend Sykes had said. His mother sat on the steps and watched them in the pool. *Someone has to keep an eye on you.* Oh, he had been a fool last spring, thinking God might disappear if men forgot to keep him in their minds. God was too big for that. And there were so many people, believing all the time. God couldn't disappear, but he might turn his head, just for a few seconds, and a terrible thing might happen. *Beware the man who by indifference dares the Lord to look away.* He might let boys at the schoolyard grab blond girls. He might let a man in cowboy boots take a knife to a blond woman. He remembered his mother on the phone: *I'm a week past due already,* she said. *What did I do to deserve this?* But people didn't get what they deserved, so Cal had to be careful. He had to keep talking to God, keep calling him. *I have not forgotten you.* The wool would remind him, like a cactus in his pants. God needed constant attention.

Cal squatted in the dark. His knees were stiff, but he didn't try to stand or stretch. Mother tapped on the closet door and invited him to dinner; he didn't answer, and she didn't insist. His father didn't stomp into the room and say, "Cut the crap, Cal."

When he emerged, Cal went straight to his bed and burrowed deep under the covers. He had the robe wadded into a ball and he curled around it, clutching it in his sleep.

Cal's mother cried out in his dreams. He saw the knife flash and heard the man say: *That'll teach you to be so choosy.* The third time she yelled Cal bolted out of bed.

He stood in the hallway outside his parents' room. Their covers were thrown back, and his mother thrashed from side to side, slapping her huge belly. "Get them off me!" she yelled. "Get them off me!" Her eyes were wide open, but she was still trapped in the dream. Cal's father put his arms around her shoulders and made her sit up. "Shush, baby," he said, "you were having a bad dream." He rocked her.

"They were crawling all over me," she said. "Look on the floor, Stan. Are they there?"

"Is what there?"

"The lizards. They were all over me."

"There aren't any lizards," Cal's father said, but he leaned down and looked under the bed just to be sure, just to humor her.

Cal had forgotten all about the lizards. He darted back to his room and dove under the bed, scrambling for the box. They were there. He counted them three times. All four of them were there, sick and slow from lack of air. It was his fault. Everything was his fault. He should never have brought them in the apartment. *I don't know what I'll do*, his mother warned. He saw her hitting her own stomach: *Get them off me.*

He tiptoed past his parents' room with the box tucked under his arm. His father was still holding her. She was calmer now, but her breath was shallow, little desperate gasps.

Cal opened the front door quietly and stepped outside. The desert air was cool; the cement was still warm. He walked a full block before he dumped the lizards on the street and watched them scurry away. He didn't want them anywhere near the apartment. A long white Cadillac cruised past, and the headlights made the pavement glitter. The driver didn't slow down. No one saw the boy on the sidewalk. Four lizards disappeared in the dark.

Some things went away and some didn't. His mother woke from her nightmare. Lizards slithered out of sight. Girls marked by a red pen scrubbed their faces clean. But Miss Faye's face was still slashed. The scar might fade but it would never go away. The leather-skinned man might go to jail, but he would never vanish. He'd crouch in his cell, panting like a dog. Any night he might break free and call to say, "I'm watching you." Maybe he'd come after her, maybe not. But even if he never called, she would hear his voice in her sleep and wake with the familiar fear.

Cal was to blame for his mother's fear. He had hidden the lizards under the bed; he had brought them into her house and into her dreams. Long after he'd set them free, Cal's mother might cry out in the night, swatting herself, sweaty and afraid.

He walked home, slowly. The stoplight flashed, a huge red eye, blinking in the dark. There were no lizards in the apartment now. His father was still cradling his mother. She rested in his arms, eyes half closed. Yes, that was something, the most anyone could ever hope for, this small comfort, one night of dreamless sleep.

In the cramped apartment with its paper walls, a quiet night must be treasured, a night without reptile dreams or visions of blond girls with marked faces, a long cool night without a child's cries. A baby might be late, but it was always born in the end. The memory of a lizard curled in the brain, ready to awaken. Cal watched his mother's huge belly rise and fall with each breath. He wanted to lay his hands on her and make it all go away; he wanted to save her from the pain. But it was much too late. Quiet nights were precious and few. Such a night might never come again.

Snake River

*M*URIEL ARNOUX DIDN'T EVEN LIKE IT, that was the shame of this whole mess. Not that she'd put up any fight. All summer long she'd watched Jay Tyler throw perfect somersaults off the high dive, leaps that made girls gasp. When the water closed around him, tears welled at the backs of Muriel's eyes, as if she'd seen him jump from the bridge over the Snake River. He surfaced, hair plastered flat, the grinning boy, and Muriel clapped, brought to ecstasy by this small miracle, a man spared by the grace of God, his body not broken on the rocks or dragged to the reservoir.

In August, a girl might cry when she imagines you've risked your life for her, but she won't like you half as much when you're parked down by the river, shivering, in November. No, in the backseat of the Chrysler, there was no clapping and no ecstasy, no double twists in layout position, no graceful entries. There were only rough hands and stubborn zippers, grunts in the dark and the terrible silence when he was done. Muriel lay there so still, Jay was afraid she wanted to be dead. *Robbing the cradle's worse than robbing the grave.* That's what Willy Hamilton said. Yeah, Jay thought, except when they're so much the same.

Plenty of girls hopped in the car with Jay Tyler. They wanted to go for ice cream or drag Main, but only one ever liked Snake River, only one ever unhooked her own bra. *Here, baby, let me help you.* Iona Moon wanted it. Too bad they never got the chance. Jay didn't have his license back then, so Willy Hamilton was at the wheel, with Belinda Beller in the front seat saying *no.* Belinda's mother was one of those women who thought boys only married virgins. *A virgin takes what you give her and doesn't complain.* Guys said it all the time. They didn't like the idea that a girl might have some basis of comparison. But when you thought about it logically, the best you could hope for was a girl who had the good sense to lie. Most guys said they'd done it and most girls said they hadn't. That meant a couple of girls were getting an awful lot of action. It was possible but not likely.

Jay wanted to explain it to Belinda Beller so she'd stop squirming and give Willy a chance, let him touch her below the neck or above the knee. Iona moaned in the backseat, and Willy said, "Time to go." Belinda got nice again and played with one of Willy's big ears, but it was too late. He popped the Chevy into reverse, and Jay and Iona almost rolled off the seat.

Iona Moon was all elbow and knee, bony ribs and hardly any breasts at all. Her dark hair smelled like damp hay, held the faint odors of the barn: cud and cow piss. Willy Hamilton was right about one thing: country girls had a dangerous grip, the strength to break a chicken's neck, and no qualms. Iona's skin was yellowish, the color of a sick baby. She was nothing to look at, but she knew what to do in the dark, and her nipples felt hard as stones in your mouth.

Muriel Arnoux had a soft belly and clean fingernails. Her hair caught the light; her skin smelled like soap. You could take a girl like Muriel home to meet your parents even though she was only fourteen. Willy Hamilton would snort over that. *Shit, Jay, you can go to jail for foolin' with a girl that age.* Sanctimonious bastard. *My father said he'd string me up by my balls if he ever heard I was baby-snatchin'.* Horton Hamilton was a man of his word. Now Willy was talking about following in his father's footsteps, being a policeman, but he was never going to fill his daddy's size twelves. Jay got a kick out of that. Good joke, but Willy didn't laugh when he heard it. Pain in the ass. Jay was glad he didn't have to depend on Willy anymore. He had his own license and his mother's car.

Jay regretted the missed chance with Iona Moon.

Her fingernails had left red marks on his back. She sucked up little pieces of flesh on his neck and he had to wear his shirts buttoned to the top for days. But she wasn't the kind of girl you wanted to eat lunch with in the cafeteria, never mind taking her home to meet your folks. She had bad teeth for one thing. *Show me a mouth like that and I'll show you a farmer's daughter.* That's what Jay's father would say, and he should know. He'd seen the insides of enough mouths. Jay knew what Andrew Johnson Tyler would say about an abortion too. He was a medical man, after all. *Nothing but a cluster of cells at this stage.* He'd pull on his pointed beard and think so hard that his hairless scalp would wrinkle halfway back his skull. *I know a doctor in Boise. Owes me a favor too.*

But it was no use thinking about what his father would say because Muriel Arnoux wasn't going to have any abortion. Jay had waited for her outside the church. She never did get up the nerve to talk to the priest. She said, "I confessed to God and he gave me his answer." Jay looked at her white ankle socks, her thin, pale calves. "I was praying, Jay, and I opened my eyes, and I saw Jesus hanging there on the cross behind the altar and he couldn't see me because his eyes were carved. Jesus has wooden eyes and he won't ever look at me again if I do this."

Jesus. Jay heard his father's words on that topic. *The Catholics drive their girls crazy, all that muttering and confessing, fondling beads and crawling into a little black booth with a priest, being forgiven so they can go out and sin again.*

*I never knew a Catholic girl who wasn't touched, half in love
with her priest or ready to die at the feet of Jesus.*

Muriel called and told him to come by at eight. "And
bring the money." Her parents had found a place for her
to stay till the baby was born. She wouldn't tell him where
it was. "Out of state," she said, "no one will know me." He
had two thousand from his grandfather in Arizona, but he
told her he only had five hundred. "Bring it all."

"You're getting off cheap," Muriel's father said. "I'd take
it out o' your hide if I had my way." He had a potbelly
and a pug nose, burly arms from loading freight for thirty
years. Muriel's mother sat in a blue armchair, blowing
her nose. The chair was covered with plastic that made
farting noises when she moved. She looked like Muriel:
all the curves turned to rolls of fat, milky skin gone pasty,
ankles swollen, but the same clean, small hands. The girl
was locked in her room, forbidden to come downstairs
while *he* was in the house. Jay imagined her, kneeling,
counting beads, seeing her Jesus nailed to the cross,
thorns piercing his scalp, eyes full of pain. *For me, Jay, he
died for me, for my sins. And look what I've done.*
 "You're never going to see my daughter again. You
understand that?"
 "Yes sir."
 "Well?"
 "Sir?"

"The money, Mr. Tyler."

Jay pulled the crumpled envelope from his pocket.

"You know how old my daughter is?"

"Yes sir, I do."

"And she's gonna have her first child. She's gonna let that baby go, and she's never gonna be the same again. Five hundred dollars just bought you your freedom, but I'll kill you and go to hell without regret if you ever come near my family again." A painting of Jesus hung over the mantel, not crucified yet, but already heavy with knowledge, his white robe parted to expose a brilliant heart. This Jesus had beautiful hands, delicate and pale, but the heart was ridiculous, the shape a child would draw and much too large.

Muriel's mother blew her nose so hard she really did fart. When he stood to go, Jay held out his hand. It was a stupid thing, something his father would do, his way of saying he understood how troublesome women could be. But Muriel's father didn't think that way. He looked at Jay's hand as if it were covered with open sores, showed him the door, and turned off the porch light before he was down the steps.

Jay knew that if he turned and looked up, he would see Muriel at the window, her nose pressed to the glass, her face already puffy. He knew she was standing with her palms flat on the pane, waiting to mouth the words: *I'm sorry, Jay.* She was sorry about everything. Sorry about being born and sorry about being female. Sorry she let him do it and sorry she didn't like it. Jay thought his father was right about Catholic girls. He didn't bother to turn around.

Months later, when he was home from the hospital, when his legs were nearly healed but the doctor said he'd have to use a cane for a year—or more—Muriel Arnoux would be sorry about that too.

"My father would whip me if he knew I was here," she said.

"You shouldn't have come."

"I had to see you, Jay."

He stared at the wall. He wanted her to go.

"I feel like I lost a part of myself," she said, "like my arm's been cut off, but the missing thing is inside."

"Yeah, well you're lucky," Jay said.

She looked at his legs, the right one still huge and heavy in the dirty cast, the left one withered and white. "I'm sorry," she said, "sometimes I'm so stupid."

"I hate it when you say that."

"When I say what?"

"Sorry. Why the fuck are you so sorry?"

"I didn't mean—"

"Forget it."

At his bedroom door, she turned. "It was a boy," she said, "if you want to know."

In the car, Jay looked at the hand Muriel's father wouldn't touch. He thought about swinging by Willy Hamilton's, saying, "You wanna go for a ride?" They'd go to the bridge and drop rocks in the river, wait for the sound, count the seconds a stone takes to fall. But they hadn't talked for months. Willy would know something was up and Jay would spill it. Then he'd have to listen to all that crap about giving a blind man a dollar in change when you owed him five, knocking over gravestones, and tipping cows when they were asleep. *I told you this would happen.* Willy Hamilton knew Jay's crimes like the fingers of his own hand: hanging from a tree to see Sharla Wilder take off her bra, telling the Wilkerson boy he could improve his thinking by drinking a cup of his own piss every day for a month, watching him down the first warm gulp, laughing so hard the tears rolled down Jay's cheeks and Roy Wilkerson knew he'd been duped. *See, you're getting smarter already.*

That was the subject of his last conversation with Willy Hamilton, back in September. *Somebody's gonna pin you to the ground someday and piss on your head, Jay Tyler. Let you know how it feels.* The lights were on in Willy's room. Horton Hamilton's cruiser was parked in the drive. *You can go to jail for foolin' with a girl that age.* Jay slowed down but didn't stop. *You just bought your freedom with five hundred dollars.*

Jay's father sat in the living room, smoking his pipe in the dark, watching television with no sound. Jay knew what that meant, knew his mother had locked herself in the bathroom upstairs. He stayed with his father, but he turned on the lights because he couldn't bear that deep, disembodied voice. No, better to see the mouth move, lips and teeth, tongue and spit, just a man after all, smoke curling from his nose.

"Man is ruled by impulse," Andrew Johnson Tyler said. "Underneath it all, we're just animals that decided to stand up."

How did he know?

"An animal is ruled by smell, really—the smell of food, the smell of a female, the smell of an enemy's fear. Instinct is stronger than reason."

Maybe they told him at the bank: Your son withdrew five hundred dollars.

"That's why every civilized society has laws. Men understand the threat of punishment. And one man is willing to punish another for the appetites he can't control in himself."

I can control myself.

"I hope your mother's life is a lesson to you, son."

He didn't know.

Now his mother was at the top of the stairs, wearing her pearls and black stockings. She clutched her beaded purse and fur stole. Jay breathed hard. He already caught a whiff of her perfume, Southern Rose spilled between her breasts, dabbed behind her ears and knees. His father packed his pipe with fresh tobacco, gave the match and those first sweet puffs his full attention. Only five more steps. She wobbled on her spike heels. Her smell filled the room.

"I'm going into town," she announced as she stood at the door. The crooked seams of her stockings meandered up her legs.

"They've done experiments with rats," Jay's father said to him. "A rat will take certain drugs until it kills itself. It will starve by choice. If you put a male and a female in the same cage, they'll fight instead of fornicate."

"Don't expect me home before dawn." His mother's voice was husky from cigarettes.

Jay and his father knew there was nowhere for her to go in White Falls, no place to dance till dawn, no place to hold your shoes in one hand while you shuffled in your stocking feet, too tired to stop. There was no place with piped-in piano music where a woman could meet a stranger, a man who whispered tender obscenities. No, there was only the saloon with the jukebox blaring, all the familiar faces, wolf whistles and propositions shouted across the bar. She wouldn't go there. *Your mother fancies herself a lady.*

After an hour, Jay saw himself walking half a mile down the road, finding his mother slumped at the wheel. He'd bring her home and help her climb the stairs, tuck the dancing shoes under her bed. An hour after that, he'd cruise down the river road, hands numb on the wheel.

"I think I'll retire," Jay's father said, knocking the ashes out of his pipe. "You should get some rest too, son." Jay nodded but didn't follow.

He waited until he heard the toilet flush before he

cracked the door and slipped outside. The night was too cold to be out without a jacket, but he didn't dare go back. He found his mother just where he thought she'd be.

"I lost the keys, baby."

"I'll look for them later, Mom."

She draped her arm over his shoulders. Her body was soft and warm. His father said she was fat, but she felt nice, a good fleshhold, hot breath on his neck, and the sweet burp of whiskey. The cold had weakened her perfume, and she smelled as she used to smell years before. Late at night, after parties or bridge, she'd come to Jay's room, lift him to the dizzy height of a dream with the scent of bruised flowers, wake him with her cool kiss and say: *Don't worry, baby, I'm home.*

They stumbled together. Black trees lined the drive, their trunks long and straight, motionless, breath sucked back, limbs frozen. The night sky swirled with the dense cloud of the Milky Way, a storm of stars, but the earth was unbearably still, strange and soundless, without wind or the rush of water, without the comfort of a car passing, that temporary light throwing long shadows, willowy human shapes. "I should've put the porch light on," Jay said. His mother clung to his arm. "I like the dark," she murmured.

She giggled at the bottom of the stairs and took off her shoes. "Don't want to wake your father."

Jay put his arm around her, his hand just below her breast.

* * *

He found the keys down the crack of the seat. He could have taken the car home, parked it in the drive, awakened in his own bed, but instead he drove toward the Snake, all the windows down, March wind blowing through his hair, the radio blasting: a pair of dueling banjos that made Jay pound the wheel. He longed to fill the night with noise, but beyond this car the only sound was the slow water of the river in late winter.

He knew every curve of the road, every bend of the river. His life eddied at the banks with the beer cans and the drowned cat. He felt the hard chest of Iona Moon, her hand on his crotch. *Time to go.* He hit sixty and felt good. He had steady hands. *I can control myself.* It didn't even last that long, didn't feel that much better than what he did alone in the bathroom—no, it was worse because Muriel lay there so still, and he had to ask, "Are you okay?" Then she looked at him as if nothing was ever going to be okay again. *Don't worry. I pulled out in time.* Iona Moon pulled the cat out of the river and tossed it up on the bank. *I've touched plenty of things that were dead longer than that.* The Chrysler could still do eighty on the highway. He pushed it to sixty-five. Muriel said, "I'm pregnant, Jay."

He raised his arms to save his eyes. She came out of nowhere, leaped onto the road as he barreled around the curve. He couldn't stop or swerve in time. The high beams of his headlights cut the night and struck her eyes, paralyzing her thin legs. Her body flopped on the hood, the most terrible sound he'd ever heard. Her small feet shattered the windshield. The car spun and the doe hit the pavement. He tried to get out of the car but he couldn't move his legs, couldn't even curl his toes without the pain shooting all the way to his skull. He didn't know if the blare in his brain was his stuck horn or his own screaming.

"Three more steps," he said. "You can make it, Mom."
She fell onto her bed, her body limp and heavy.
"Do you think I'm pretty, Jay?"
Your mother dresses like a whore.
"You look nice, Mom."
"Not too fat?"
Puffed up like Marilyn Monroe.
"No, Mom, you look fine."
She was an alcoholic too, you know.
She patted the soft bulge of her belly. "I used to have a flat stomach, but having you took care of that. That doctor your father knows in Boise wrecked my muscles cutting you out. Stitched me up like the Bride of Frankenstein too. I should have sued, but your father said he couldn't do that to a friend, another man of medicine. Easy for him to say. It wasn't his belly."
"I know, Mom, you told me."
"He was a butcher."
"Yes, you should have sued."

"My daddy said I was the prettiest girl in White Falls. I could have had any boy I wanted and look what I got."

Jay's right leg was broken in three places, his left in one. Shards of the windshield had cut his arms and hands, but his eyes were spared.

"You broke your own legs," the doctor said, trying to offer some comfort or lay the proper blame. "You would've been all right if you'd just relaxed. I've seen it before. People punch the brakes and go rigid. Just your luck to have such strong thighs."

"Yeah," Jay said, "I'm a lucky guy."

"Any boy I wanted and I end up with a man who hates me."

"He doesn't hate you, Mom."

"Lie down next to me, Jay. I caught a chill out there in the car." He stretched out beside her on the bed. "Just keep me warm till I fall asleep." She wasn't cold at all, but he stayed. "You know what they did to me when your father sent me to that clinic in Wharton, that *spa* for worrisome wives?"

"You told me, Mom."

"Did I tell you I thought I was blind?"

"Yes."

"I thought the bones of my legs had splintered."

"Yes, I remember."

" 'Just a little jolt, Mrs. Tyler. This won't hurt at all.' But they put a piece of rubber in your mouth so you won't break your own teeth. They know and they do it anyway."

"Sssh, Mom, don't think about it. Just go to sleep."

"I heard my spine crack."

Jay put his arms around her. "You're safe now."

"The blood in my head boiled; I could hear it burning my brain. The doctor said, 'One more time.' That's when I died, Jay. I swear to you I died. When I woke up, I kept thinking about your father and your grandfather, walking me up the steps, one on each side, the last day of my life. I looked at your father's father, his face tanned and wrinkled, his teeth too white when he grinned. I said, 'Please don't leave me here,' and he said, 'There now, be a good girl, Delores, and don't put up a fuss.' "

Jay waited for a disaster, an avalanche or a flood, a search for survivors that would make his father turn up the sound on the television. He wished his mother would get out of bed and knock on his door, so he could hear himself say: *Leave me alone.* Any day, he thought, a car will turn in the drive, just by mistake.

The grass grew greener. Leaves unfurled. One night, he broke his dinner plate, flung it across the room, saw it splinter against the wall. The sound shattered the air, but no one ran to his room and nothing changed. His father and his grandfather still walked his mother up the steps; he still had Muriel Arnoux pinned to the backseat of the Chrysler. When he closed his eyes, the doe leaped out of the woods. He saw her dark, startled gaze, her thin legs. *Why didn't she run?* He slammed on the brakes, but there was no way to stop.

Sites

*P*EOPLE STILL THINK MY sister killed a man. At parties, women bend their heads together, nodding in my direction. Lies seem more true when they're whispered. Men I barely know watch me all night, searching for the flush of Grace's fever in my cheeks. Terrified and awed by the promise of our common blood, they almost love me. But fear is a beguiler, a mimic of lust. When one grows bold enough to ask to drive me home, he is inevitably disappointed. I can satisfy neither curiosity nor desire. The story of the night Grace stabbed a man in Boston's Combat Zone only has power if I don't tell it, and my sister's summer storms run cool in me, the drizzle of winter rain.

Even among our relatives, Grace inspires lies. My

aunt Dee has claimed for years that she saw Grace spit in our father's grave the day he was buried. This is utterly false, though it is true that Gracie did not cry at the funeral.

My tears were few but real, despite Grace's accusation that I blinked until my eyes watered. Grace missed the actual funeral, and I didn't expect her at the burial either, but then she appeared, skinnier than I had ever seen her, wearing a black leather miniskirt and black fishnet stockings, a pillbox hat with mesh that fell over her eyes that she must have dug up in some ratty secondhand shop, a sleeveless black T-shirt and no bra. Gracie, the bereaved in mourning clothes.

While the minister did his ashes-to-ashes speech, I felt Gracie fidgeting behind me; she kept stooping and I heard her bad knee crack. The familiar pop of my sister's bones gave me an odd sense of comfort. I imagined her twisting a handkerchief, dropping it again and again in silent distress. But when the preacher had had his say, I turned and saw Grace's true purpose: she had gathered up a whole fistful of dandelions, and now she clutched them as if she expected them to writhe away.

Mom glanced over her shoulder and shot Gracie a smile from the half of her face that still worked. "Glad you could make it, Grace," she said and didn't wait for an answer.

"My sympathies to you too, Mother," Grace sputtered, close to my ear.

Mom threw a white rose into the open grave, and it

slapped the box like a small, limp body. Uncle Eddie rolled Granny's wheelchair up to the edge and she tossed a handful of purple pansies from her own garden. But they fell short and Uncle Eddie had to get down on his hands and knees to gather them up and pitch them down the hole. His sluggishness irritated my grandmother; she would have kicked him if she'd had the strength. Her gnarled hands beat against fleshless thighs and her mouth was pulled tight, a wrinkled red *oh* of complete disgust. She was eighty-three, crippled by arthritis, with bones so porous they might wash away in a hard rain, but her mind was mercifully—or cruelly—as sharp as it had ever been. "I don't waste blood on my legs," she once said to me. "Who needs to walk at my age? Certainly not a woman with a forty-two-year-old son who never married. What good is such a boy if he can't take an old woman where she wants to go?" She said this right in front of Uncle Eddie; but he didn't protest, he only stared at his thick white toes wiggling in his sandals.

Aunt Dee, Daddy's older sister, cast a dozen lilies, one by one. "Show-off," Gracie hissed behind me. "I bet she's pissed he kicked in summer—can't wear your mink in July." But Aunt Dee didn't appear to be suffering without her furs. She had a new rock on her finger, a twenty-fifth anniversary present from my absent uncle Philip. "I guess Phil didn't want to mingle with the commoners," Grace said. "There's nothing worse than showing up at the wrong man's funeral." Aunt Dee's diamond caught a ray of sunlight and shot sparks of yellow fire.

The preacher was about to heave the first clod of dirt when Gracie stepped forward and flicked her dandelions into the shallow pit. I hope I was the only one near enough to hear her mutter, "Something sweet to smell, Daddy."

In the limousine, I sat between Grace and my mother. We hadn't made it to the bottom of the hill before Gracie dug a vial of white powder out of her purse. The top had a miniature spoon on a hinge. She scooped out the pale dust and held it to one nostril and then the other, snorting hard. Mom sobbed. "Don't you have any respect?" she said.

"Daddy doesn't care."

"I do."

"I'm grief-stricken, Mother, nearly paralyzed with pain. Let me comfort myself as I choose."

I put my arm around my mother. There was no sense in trying to keep Grace from doing or saying what she pleased, so I didn't. But I thought she could pick her words more carefully, and it made me sad looking at my mother's useless right arm, curled against her like a shrunken wing. I would have kissed her, but I was on the wrong side; I couldn't bear to press my lips against the sagging skin of her numb cheek.

"It's not fair," Mom said, "he's been so good."

"Two years on the wagon doesn't make up for twenty years in the gutter."

"Your father wasn't a bum."

"No, that's true," Grace said, her voice sharp as the flickering edge of a shattered windowpane. "No, he was no street slime, no sewer rat. He drank at home, where we would all enjoy his fine company."

Mom said, "He's been an angel. You don't know."

"Can't live without a liver," Grace said, cold and exact.

I thought Grace was too hard on our father—even though he did force her to marry that pockmarked, sullen boy when she was only sixteen, even though he did forbid her to ever enter his house again after the night she made off with Mother's amethyst earrings and a strand of pearls we'd been told were real. They weren't, but they had belonged to Mother's mother, that much was true. Mom scoured Boston's pawnshops and paid fifty dollars for the string of beads, twice what they were worth. The earrings were forever lost.

"People shouldn't be so attached to things," Gracie said when I delivered the message that she was not to set foot in our parents' house again.

"People shouldn't steal," I said. "People should honor their father and mother."

"Oh, *please*," said Grace.

My sister has always lived by her own code; she even takes pride in her sense of honor. She would never read your mail. She would not use your last scoop of coffee or wear your clothes without asking. She would take punishment before she would name another as the guilty party. I know this because she bent over Daddy's knee for my whipping when I set fire to the living room drapes and was too young and cowardly to confess.

The trouble between Grace and my father actually began long before she stole the pearls. Even as a child Grace seemed to delight in tormenting Dad, though she was always the one to suffer in the end. I do not know whether she considered annoyance an art or if she fell into her aggravating ways by accident. I do know she was fearless in the face of Dad's fury, and this gave her a strange power. His knuckles white with rage, his face red enough to pop, our 195-pound father would threaten to drive Grace's head through the wall if she uttered another word. Though she might have nothing left to say, my frail sister would never fail to speak that last word. And yet she lived. I considered this a miracle and regarded Grace with secret reverence.

Still, there were battles where she spat out dangerous words and did not win. I remember the April day when Gracie was caught necking with Gordon Haddow, our seventeen-year-old neighbor. Gordon had slanted eyes and big feet that dragged when he walked as if they were a burden, too heavy for his legs. He mumbled three-word sentences and never went to school, but Grace didn't mind and had been his best friend since she was five and Gordon let her watch him pee.

The circumstances of their romantic explorations were peculiar. At the border of the Haddows' yard where juniper bushes grew thick against the high fence, Gordon and Grace dug a cave in the ground and crawled inside for an afternoon of delight. Hours later when Mrs. Haddow found them and pulled them out of the hole, they both giggled and rolled on the grass, feeble from lack of oxygen.

Of course Grace was blamed, even though she was still a month shy of thirteen. Everyone understood that poor Gordon didn't know any better, but that Grace certainly did.

At dinner Mom was silent and Dad reminded my sister that she wasn't too old to have her pants pulled down and her fanny thrashed. "You could have died," he said.

Grace, cool and womanly even at twelve, asked: "What bothers you more, Daddy? That I could have died or that I spent all day smooching with Gordon Haddow?"

Dad stuttered. A vision of the hulking, clumsy boy wavered in front of him. He said, "One more word out of you . . ."

"You don't have such great taste yourself, Daddy."

Dad's ears blazed and I waited for steam.

Mom said, "What the hell is that supposed to mean?"

"Not you, Mom, I don't mean you. I mean that cow-eyed bimbo with the huge tits. What do you call her? Your *receptionist*?"

"She does a good job," Mom said.

Dad's right hand was raised, as if he'd reached for his glass of milk and turned to stone.

Grace stared at Mother. "Don't you know?" she said.

For ten seconds no one moved or spoke. My father's hand still hung in the air and a ridiculous smirk twisted his mouth. Then my mother exploded, snatching plates half loaded with food off the table. She tossed them in the sink without scraping them, ran water, and squirted soap until peas and globs of mashed potatoes floated to the scummy surface. "Of course I know," she said at last, and my father's hand crashed against the table.

Grace was sixteen when she obeyed my father for the last time. She was pregnant, and my parents insisted on the decency of ritual. I loathed my brother-in-law, that scarred, stubby boy who always had the sand of sleep at the corners of his eyes. At thirteen, I was a heartless judge. But now I know something good came of this brief union, a daughter who makes me believe that Grace and I are not entirely alone in the world. No, somewhere there is a girl, the child of Grace's childhood. We do not even know her name, such are the rules that govern adoption, but I would recognize her anywhere. Like Grace, she has dimples in her knees instead of her cheeks, wispy hair that burns with gold flames at the end of summer. She never stands straight, and her mother, not the real one, constantly reminds her to stop slouching and to take her hands off her hips, until little Grace (I call her that) sighs in exasperation and says *oh please* as she stomps out of the room, hands plunged deep in pockets, back defiantly curved.

*   *   *

My friends think I must resent my sister for all the trouble she's caused me. Even Claudia Reinhart, who is my oldest friend and claims to understand what's best for me, thinks I should move and get an unlisted number so Gracie can't call me in the middle of the night to rescue her from the police station in Tewksbury or some phone booth that she thinks is about ten miles south of Haverhill.

Claudia says she wants to spare me from the stress and expense of midnight missions with bail money. Perhaps her concern for me is genuine, but Claudia's quarrel with Grace is thirteen years old and goes back to the time Grace referred to her as "that pudgy midget."

Claudia is forever remaking herself, dyeing her hair or waxing her legs, plucking her brows or sanding her cheeks with pumice stones, eating nothing but grapefruit one week and nothing but tuna the next.

And Claudia is forever falling in love "for the first time." She says, "I mean it, this is the first time I've *really* been in love." Then she disappears from my life only to emerge two weeks later, eating chocolate and swearing she will never, never trust another man as long as she lives.

She maintains that Grace is responsible for destroying my "one chance for happiness with a man." Richard Egerton and I had finally moved in together after our senior year at Northeastern. This was three years after Grace stabbed a man in the Zone, and I hadn't seen my sister for fourteen months. Some friends of hers thought she'd gone out to San Francisco. I felt giddy, lightened by the knowledge of distance between us.

Richard and I had spent two years tossing in each other's arms without giving in to temptation. He had some archaic beliefs about sex sapping your strength and killing off brain cells. When things got dangerous, he rolled over on his belly and pounded the sheets with his fists.

I was tolerant. I let him keep his gaunt, pale body chaste. I watched him sweat over history papers instead of me. I believed in his future and his need to preserve his precious energy during exams. But on graduation day, with Richard safely accepted at Suffolk Law School, I gave him an ultimatum and we moved into a tiny two-room apartment in Cambridge, where I discovered that in some cases deprivation is preferable to fulfillment.

My degree was in psychology, but I took a job with a law firm downtown, pretending I had plans to go to law school. I wanted to justify my years of frustration with Richard; I wanted the two of us to fit together. Bigelow and Dropkin specialized in malpractice. My task was to dig through files for cases similar to the ones they were handling; I filtered out the best examples and arranged them in order of ascending importance to establish the power of precedent. This saved Bigelow and Dropkin from spending too much time toying with capricious juries; they did most of their work over lunch and martinis, using my research to bargain with the defendants' lawyers. I was good at this job because it all made so little difference to me.

The summer had almost ended when Gracie knocked at our door, blown in by the wind from the west, golden and glowing, her hair hennaed a brilliant red, her body slim and firm, not yet sunken in the chest or knobby at the joints.

I felt fat and white standing beside her, my hair colorless as stagnant water, my thighs loose with flesh. She was a goddess, my dark-eyed sister; the vast difference was not lost on Richard.

I could easily claim Grace seduced him, led him astray, transfixed him with her false beauty, but that would be a lie. I saw him follow her around the apartment, a dog on her heels. I saw him reach out and touch her hair, so lightly she could not feel his fingertips.

I didn't have to catch them together or anything so crude. I only had to come home one evening and find the apartment ransacked and Richard sitting in the middle of the floor, weeping into his hands. She had taken eighty-five dollars, two pounds of sugar, and Richard's diamond cuff links, a graduation gift from his mother. The mess was just for effect.

Telling Richard I would buy him another, identical pair of cuff links only made his wailing worse: they would not be *the* pair his mother had given him.

Claudia uses this as an example of one of the many ways Grace has tried to ruin my life. Of course I left a few details out of the version of the story I told my friend. She imagines Gracie stole the cuff links simply because they were the most valuable item in the apartment, and she could hock them for a hundred and score a gram of coke. Only I know Gracie's revenge was tribal, calculated to punish Richard for his unfaithfulness to me. Only I know this was Grace's way of saving me from years of misery with the wrong man.

I tell Claudia, "She's my sister," as if this explains everything.

Most times, Grace finds me when she wants company, but there was one occasion, one hot October in the flash of Indian summer, when I tracked her to a dive off Washington Street, a place called, cryptically, The End. On the sign, neon flashed: Girls Girls Girls. I would have let it lie when I heard what Grace was doing, but Mom had just had her first stroke, and I felt honor-bound to find my sister.

I cruised in at five; the joint was empty but already stale with smoke and thick with windowless gloom. I sat down at the bar and the tender said, "Let's see some ID, little lady." I was nineteen.

"I'm looking for my sister," I said.

"Aren't we all."

I pulled out a picture of Grace, an old one, when her tightly permed hair emphasized the unusual length of her skinny neck. The bartender studied it. He was thick in the chest and his head seemed to sink into his burly shoulders;

his hair was shaved flat on top. He reminded me of an overdeveloped marine. "No way," he said, chuckling.

"It's an old picture," I told him, "look again."

He shook his head. "That girl's an old maid somewhere in Ohio by now."

"I heard she was here."

"Trust me."

I asked him when the show started and thanked him for his help. "Bring some ID," he yelled as I swung through the door.

That night, I sat through two sets: through Golden Glory, a peroxide blonde decked out in yellow feathers and a sequined G-string. She twirled up and down the runway, feathers floating around her. She fell to her knees and then her back, body twitching, feathers fluttering like the wings of a wounded bird, a canary made hideous by its size. The final thrill came when she flung the G-string over her head and revealed a bleached triangle of frizzy curls. Something about pale hair in unexpected places drives men to hoot and growl. But their boredom surprised me; the sounds seemed gratuitous, and they didn't care when the yellow girl vanished.

A fleshy redhead dressed as a cowgirl peeled away a ruffled skirt and popped her corset. She pranced, cavorting in nothing but her garter, stockings, boots and spurs. The strip was fast, the tease nonexistent.

The entrance of the next girl—Domina—provoked a few lazy wolf whistles. She strutted. She scowled. She

spun on her three-inch spike heels. Her eyes were lined
in black, made up to look long and slanted beneath the
thick bangs of her dark wig. She wore a studded cat
collar, a black leather bra with rhinestone nipples, leather
shorts, and gloves that came past her elbows. Her whip
cracked the air, and a man near the runway pretended he
wanted to climb up and let her step on his head with
those spiked boots. She sneered and would have been
glad to accommodate him, I thought.

She stalked through a whole tune without shedding
a stitch, but when the second song crackled through the
speakers, men slapped the bar with their palms and
chanted. The gloves rolled off first and a silky silver
G-string fell last. As the girl scurried between the curtains to the final beats of the music, she'd lost the bold-
ness of Domina and was just bare-assed Grace. Even the
men must have sensed the fraud: in the long silent seconds before the next throb of drums, they sat still and
numb, sipping their drinks, polite as church boys.

I made my way backstage fast enough to hear a
man's low voice say, "She better develop some love for
her work."

Gracie and Golden Glory were passing a joint between them when I opened the dressing room door.
"What the fuck?" the blonde said.

Gracie pulled the black wig off her head and ran her
fingers through her flattened hair. It was cropped short
and frosted. She had a red kimono wrapped around her,
but it gaped open and I could see her naked breasts and

white belly. "Shit," she said. "You shouldn't have come here."

"You know this baby face?" said the yellow woman.

"My sister."

"Looking for a job, baby sister?" The blonde gagged when she said it, choking on the weed.

"Get out of here," Gracie said. She glared at me, but I didn't budge. I had a mission; I could afford to be stubborn. "You heard me," she said, "move your ass." My feet were stuck to the floor, set in concrete, dragging me to the bottom of the river.

"Mind the lady," Blondie said, "before we get some *assistance*."

"I mean you, Marlene," Grace said, finally, looking at the peroxide princess. "Give us some space."

The blonde uncrossed her legs and snorted. "Yeah," she said, "glad to oblige, but the reefer's mine." She snatched the roach out of Grace's mouth. "Meet you on the funway," she said, brushing past me.

"Bitch," Grace muttered.

"Mom's sick," I said. I thought I'd spare us both the small talk.

"What else is new?"

"No, not like that—for real this time. You better see her." I told her about the stroke. If she was concerned, she didn't say so, and she didn't ask for many particulars. But she had one cigarette burning in the ashtray, one going on the edge of the counter, and another in her mouth by the time I was done with my story.

"I've got one more set," she said at last.

"More whips?"

"No, a little-girl routine, pigtails and all, Mary, Mary, quite contrary. Cheap joint. They pass me off as a fresh girl."

"Tomorrow?" I said.

"Sure," she said, "tomorrow."

But Gracie never made it to the hospital because that was the night she put a paring knife through a man's hand and got sent to the women's prison in Framingham.

Our father wouldn't bail her out, and I had to go around to all our friends, scraping dollars and dimes, which is how the rumor got started that Grace killed a man.

It took me six days to get the money together; Grace was getting a bad rap—she'd severed a tendon in the man's hand and paralyzed two fingers. He had a story that she'd held the blade to his throat and threatened to slit him cheek to cheek before she coolly plunged the knife into his hand.

Grace denied this version of the story and claimed it was strictly an act of passion. Dudes could buy a dancer a drink for six bucks, and this guy, Mickey Moss, forty-five, married, and the father of four, was buying Grace her third gin and tonic when he started to think that eighteen dollars should be getting him more than conversation, especially since Gracie's half of the conversation consisted mainly of "yes" and "no" and came down heavy on the *no* side. She slapped his right hand away from her knee, knocked it away from her butt, told him flat out she didn't mess with customers, but he wouldn't believe her. That's when he clutched her tit and wouldn't let go, and that's when she grabbed the paring knife that Al the bartender had left behind after he cut extra lime for her tonic. She brought it down on the man's left hand and he pinched her breast so hard with his right that he made five fingerprints, deep purple bruises that were photographed in leering color and used as evidence.

Even so, the jury didn't have much regard for the virtue of a dancer called Domina who wore a cat collar and a leather bra. Her lawyer tried to make the ten women on the jury sympathize with her outrage, remember being fondled at a party or tweaked at work. But the women resented the comparison; they had nothing in common with a trashy stripper from the Zone. The lawyer's tactics turned the women against Grace in the end. She never did have half a chance with the two men, who sat through the trial with their arms crossed over their chests, their hands tucked safely under their biceps.

Gracie got two years and served six months. The first time I saw her in prison she said, "Thank God Mom had her stroke *before* this happened. Otherwise she'd blame it on me." I nodded and didn't tell her that Mom blamed her anyway, holding Grace responsible for all the years she'd spent fretting over her wayward daughter.

I was the only one in the family to visit Grace at Framingham. I tried to make excuses for the others, but

Grace covered her ears. We sat together in a bare room. A guard stood five feet away, hearing everything, responding to nothing. Grace wanted to talk about her lovers. It kept her sane to think about sex, she said, and besides, she knew how *deprived* I was. If she didn't tell me, how would I ever know anything? I told her I wasn't as deprived as she thought, but fortunately she didn't urge me to elaborate.

She liked variety and preferred men who couldn't speak much English. "It's easier," she said, "if you don't have to bother with conversation." She'd had two Arabs, an eighty-year-old Chinese grandfather, a Colombian dealer, and three Native Americans. "I like to do my part for the Indians," she said. "They got a bum deal from us."

But her most recent affair, one that hadn't quite ended before her bad luck in the Zone, was with a 352-pound man named Harry. "It's amazing," she said, "his *finger* barely fits in my mouth. I mean the man is *fat*."

"Aren't you afraid he'll crush you? Didn't Fatty Arbuckle kill some girl that way?"

"That's why it's so great. He's scared to death of hurting me and I always get to be on top. It's like making love to a whale, all that blubber, and me bouncing up and down; you never saw so much flesh. He'd die if he heard me say this, but I forget he's even there—it's not like being with a person—it's like fucking a giant jellyfish. I keep thinking he'll swallow me whole when we're done, that there's a huge mouth hidden in his belly, one gulp and I'll be gone."

"Sounds great," I said. She thought I meant it.

"There's only one problem."

"I can't imagine."

"He smells."

"Most of us do."

"Not like this. He can't get really clean, you know. All that fat. Sweats like a beast. He'd be lifting folds all day long to rinse everything away. So he doesn't bother—just a quick dip in the shower. I tried to get in with him once to give him a good soaping, but there wasn't room."

"Nobody's perfect," I said.

"Ever been with a dwarf?"

"Don't tell me." I meant it. I didn't want to hear this story.

"Neither have I," she said, "but I was with a guy with one leg once."

"Your time's up," the guard said.

"I'm almost through."

"Time's up." He wouldn't bargain. He was short and flabby; a gold band squeezed his thick finger. I wondered if he smelled. I wondered if his wife forgot he was a person when they made love.

When our father died, Grace had been out of prison for three years and banned from the house for eight, but she still knew our parents. She said, "Mom will be lucky to last a year without the old bugger to run her ragged. She lives to be his slave." Grace overestimated. It took our mother four months to give up and cut herself loose. Another stroke sent her reeling away from us for the last time.

She walked somewhere high and light without words, a world I could only imagine when I sat beside her and watched the first flurries of winter spin by the window. Her lids fluttered with dreams and secret visions. Sometimes I entered the room and her eyes were flung open, blue and brilliant, fearful or amazed. I'd hold her good hand, stroking the palm, uncurling the clamped claws of her fingers. I talked and talked but her look never changed; I could not share her joy or make her less afraid.

It took me three days and sixty-two phone calls to track Grace. When she finally stumbled into the hospital, I wished I hadn't tried so hard. She was bony and broke, strung out on speed because she didn't have the cash for cocaine. Nincty-nine pounds stretched over her five-seven frame. She smoked incessantly and answered no questions. She cussed at the nurses and told the doctor to eat shit when he said she could smoke only in the lounge.

The bags under her eyes were so black I thought she'd taken two punches. Her left eye twitched, her feet beat out a frenzied tap on the tile floor, she cracked her knuckles, chewed gum and kept smoking.

In my head, I heard my mother's voice again and again, always the same words, the ones she had said to me just a week before the stroke: *Take care of Gracie when I'm gone. You're the only one who could ever make her listen.*

But that was a lie. Gracie never listened to anyone as far as I knew. Still, this was my mother's last request. I wanted to find some sense in it because she'd made it solemnly, as if she saw the closeness of her future, the future of this white room, with one tube pumping fluids into her and another sucking liquids out.

Before she died, there would be other tubes, first in her nostrils and then in her throat, finally one in her chest to drain the thick yellow pus that threatened to drown her. But Gracie would be long gone before she had to see any of that.

My father's relatives made their final obligatory visit two days before Thanksgiving. Gran insisted on being rolled to the very edge of the bed, where she could poke at a balled-up fist or look inside Mother's open mouth. I thought of the time I had seen my grandmother use her wheelchair to back Mom into a corner of the kitchen. The old woman railed and spat on the floor, blaming my mother for her son's wasted life. "He never drank in my house," Gran said, inching her chair forward till her footrest pressed against Mom's shins. "I wouldn't allow it."

Gran also held my mother solely responsible for getting pregnant before Dad finished college. "He could have been a dentist," Gran said, though Dad had never shown any special interest or talent for such a profession. "And instead he sells life insurance, harbinger of death, making money off strangers' fear and swearing over their sorrows."

Aunt Dee brought tulips to the hospital. They sprang from the glass vase, their heads bright and furious, so red they seemed to excite the air. But even the assault of the delirious flowers could not stir my mother. Dee leaned over the bed and yelled, "You look fine today, honey, just fine, a regular beauty. You'll be dancing by next week."

"Yeah, on her own grave," Uncle Eddie murmured. Gran slapped his thigh and Mother blinked, hearing the mumbled truth more clearly than the compliments Dee shouted in her face.

On Thanksgiving, Mom said: *Gracie doesn't have anyone but you.* I snapped awake, cramped from sleeping in the chair, a bad taste in my mouth from the sticky potatoes and gravy I'd eaten in the hospital cafeteria. My mother had left the room. Only her body remained, that fragile sack of skin and bone shackled by tubes and bags. She was free at last and had stopped just long enough to whisper those words in my ear. They were true. My mother was an only child, and both her parents were dead. My father's family couldn't wait to forget their connection to me and Grace, the orphaned daughters.

I couldn't find my sister. It was seven months before she heard Mom was dead.

Perhaps I would have mourned more deeply for my mother if she hadn't left me such a mess of affairs. Everything was in my name: the house, the car, the costume jewelry. But as I dug through the yellowed papers of my parents' lives, I discovered they had bequeathed a startling array of hidden debts to me as well: there was a second mortgage on the house, unpaid hospital bills after my father's health insurance was canceled, and a persistent pile of bills from a car accident after his car insurance was canceled. I found that notice too: Termination due to seven claims and five speeding tickets in one year. He sold insurance but couldn't hang on to his own. He'd cashed in his life insurance policy six years before he died; Mom cashed in her policy to have him buried. I took a week off from work, and then an indefinite leave of absence, but I knew I could not go back to Bigelow and Dropkin, to the senseless job I found vaguely dishonorable. I had paid my dues for my wretched affair with Richard, and I finally admitted I had no intention of going to law school.

It took me six months to sort out the mess and sell the house; by the time the accounts were settled, I had less than two thousand dollars, a crumpled Toyota riddled with rust, and a rhinestone brooch. Other children might have resented such a paltry legacy, but on the June morning when I paid the last bill and signed the final papers on the house, I felt weightless, a bag full of air, and I mistook this unexpected lightness for the pure joy of my new freedom.

With the two thousand in the bank and the brooch stuffed safely in the toe of a sock in my suitcase, I climbed in my beat-up blue Toyota and headed north for a week in a shack on the coast of Maine, where the weight returned. Like a body I dragged behind me, my burden bloated. Day by day it grew heavier and more foul. It tugged my legs through the dark, endless nights as the stars of the Milky Way swirled above me. I made up names for the constellations I saw: The Wild Boar, The Headless Horse, The Two Sisters.

I was grateful for the familiar smog of Boston, the strangely vacant night sky, where only the brightest stars survived and did not spin into dizzy shapes. Claudia offered to let me stay with her until "I got myself together," but she fell in love. The walls of her cramped studio on Beacon Street seemed to bulge with so many bodies, the fresh body of Claudia's infatuation and the fetid corpses of my waking dreams. She gave me a week.

In the middle of Boston's worst heat wave of the summer, I found myself looking for a job and an apartment. The sticky July air made the thought of a real job, one that required stockings and a clean face, unbearable. When the days were crisp and brief, I'd be able to think; I'd get a job in my field and stop wasting my education. But now all I needed was money: fast, regular rolls of cash.

I landed a night shift in a fish house on the waterfront, a tourist joint with nets hanging on the walls and lobster traps dangling from the ceiling. I sublet a sweltering, roach-infested studio apartment on Park Drive, believing, I suppose, that the punishment of my surroundings at work and at home would be a constant reminder of the necessity of finding a real job in September.

I should have sensed that I was creating the perfect environment for Grace to resurface.

She was slumped in my entryway when I got home from work at two o'clock one Sunday morning. I spotted her as soon as I started up the walkway and had no doubts, no fleeting illusion that some street person had crashed in the foyer, though strangers occasionally drifted here from the Fenway and spent the night if no one hauled them out to the curb. But there was no mistake: the tilt of the head was undeniably my sister's.

"Shit," she said when I shook her shoulder. She rubbed her eyes and scrambled to her feet. "I thought you'd never get here."

She'd gained ten pounds but was still skinny. Her hair was shaved down to half an inch and bleached an icy blond. Her stockings were ripped, and she couldn't remember where she'd lost her shoes.

I spent a week trying to fatten her up, feeding her burgers and fried potatoes, the only foods she craved. Late at night when I came home smelling of clam juice and spilled beer, I'd find Grace sprawled on the couch, her half-eaten burger dropped on the floor beside her, dripping ketchup onto the carpet.

She always woke, apologizing for the mess but making no effort to clean it up. We drank from jugs of cheap white wine and Grace told me stories.

The last night she was there, she told me about her

German lover, an actor she'd met in New York, a man who hadn't been home in twenty years, who never wrote his mother and father and had ceased to acknowledge his brother was his blood. He left Kiel the summer his brother had tried to drown him. For months he had begged to ride in the kayak, and at last, in the white blaze of afternoon, the older boy took him out on the Baltic. They paddled hard, skimming the choppy surface, noticing too late the clouds foaming in the western sky. The scud snuffed out the sun, turned the sea black and wild with rain. They fought the waves, beating their way back to shore. With safety in sight, the older boy began to rock and laugh, pitching left and right, harder and faster until he swamped the kayak. He easily freed himself, but the younger boy panicked. Trapped in the dark silent water where the wind stopped and the waves opened, he saw his brother's slow thighs, treading water above him. It was a lesson: *Now you don't have to be afraid of anything.* And he wasn't, but he never went home.

Grace said, "Can you imagine, trying to drown your own brother?" I shook my head as if it was unfathomable, but I have felt my own head go under, my lungs filling with water; I have beat my way to the surface and seen my sister laughing on a distant shore.

"He was the best lover I ever had," Grace said, "but I had to give him up. He scared me. He didn't believe in anything."

We drank until the stagnant light before dawn filled the room. I downed far more than I usually did, or more

264

than I ever should. Gracie seemed to match me glass for glass, but perhaps she fooled me, because as the room blurred and spun, I saw that her dark eyes glowed until they burned, two golden flames. When the streetlights dimmed, Grace's eyes were the only beacons in the world.

I dreamed of my sister holding my head under water. Unlike the German boy, Grace did not tread water above me or swim toward shore. No, they found us together, face down in the muck at the bottom of a shallow pond, arms and legs entwined, heads bent together, our hair tangled in the flowing reeds.

I woke in a heap on the floor, my skin imprinted by the scratchy tufts of the carpet, my tongue swollen and dry, my teeth fuzzy. Grace was gone. At least she was neat this time. She didn't tear the place apart to find my cash. She must have seen me stuff my tips in an envelope between the plastic liner and the cardboard box of the Raisin Bran. My week's earnings, two hundred and thirty-seven dollars, was the only thing she took.

This time I couldn't convince myself that it was for my own good. I hadn't seen Richard for two years, but I felt close to him now and knew at last why he wept so inconsolably over his stolen cuff links. I brushed my teeth, standing at the window instead of the mirror, tears rolling down my cheeks.

I know it's crazy, but I am hoping that when Grace's daughter is old enough to want to meet her mother,

Grace will be impossible to find. That's not hard to imagine. I think of the little girl knocking at my door instead—of course she won't be little anymore, but halfway to womanhood, her neck still too long for her to have learned to use it as Grace uses hers, stretching and arching so men dream of putting their hands around it, not too tightly, pressing their lips to her white skin. And I will tell a small lie, for all of us. I will say I changed my first name to hide from her abusive father. I will say I am her mother. I will live with Grace's name and take this child away, north, to Alaska, where Grace, who hates the cold, will never find us. I will be free at last, and not alone. Often, I curse our common name—Walker. That child will be a long time looking for us.

On New Year's Eve, Grace reappeared. "I wanted to celebrate with my sister," she said. She had forgotten the circumstances of her abrupt departure. She'd spent a month in detox and was straight for the first time since she'd been in prison. She had a job, she said, "sales," and then admitted, "selling muffins in Harvard Square." I told her I was going to a party at Claudia's, hoping she'd curl her lip in distaste. But she surprised me; she wanted to go. When she was off the dope, she didn't have any friends of her own. I thought of telling her that Claudia didn't trust her in her apartment, but Grace would have made me choose between them.

An hour before the party, my sister found me this way: sobbing my fool head off in the bathtub. She didn't ask why; she just put her arms around me—even though she was ruining the red silk blouse she planned to wear to the party. I would have considered this a great sacrifice except the shirt was mine.

She said, "I hope you aren't thinking of drowning yourself. I was thinking of that one day, just slipping down in the tub, letting myself go, you know, an accident. Then last week I was feeling fine; three weeks in detox and I'm a new person. I have a real life, you know, like anyone else. And I'm feeling so good that while I'm washing my hair, kneeling and leaning under the faucet, I get rambunctious and bring my head down so fast that I bash it against the end of the tub. I see constellations. I think, oh great, I'm going to have a real accident and everyone will say I did it on purpose, that they expected it sooner or later. They'll find me face down, ass up. God, I thought, I don't want to die with my bare ass in the air for the world to see."

The thought of her naked bum made us howl and shake, spouting giggles till I thought we'd burst, and Grace hugged me tighter and tighter until I was crying again and she had to say, "What is it, baby?"

But how could I explain? Mom had always told us, "Don't get married on a holiday. You get divorced and you can never forget the fourth of July, but May seventeenth—who remembers May seventeenth?" So wasn't it just like Mom to die on Thanksgiving, so I'd remember? Well, maybe she didn't choose the day, any more than a child chooses her day to be born. If Grace wasn't crying today, why should I remind her that this was her daughter's eleventh birthday, her daughter, our blood. Why should I tell her that I woke this morning and said to myself: *She'll never find us. And if she has any sense, she'll never even look.*

I should have been happy. Grace was straight and had a job. She was going to make it this time. So what whispering devil made me hide my rings; what demon of doubt drove me to make a special trip to the bank to deposit all my cash?

Claudia and I have kept our New Year's resolutions. It is spring in Boston and we both have new jobs. I've moved to Somerville, to a barren apartment where there is room to pace and no cockroaches to chase when you flick on the bathroom light in the middle of the night. Leaf buds have burst like green flames and the forsythia are painfully yellow.

I stop at Claudia's apartment on my way home. She is down on love this week. It's her day off and she's gone through a bag of chocolate cookies. She says that when she feels fat, the desire goes away. She's landed a job doing makeup for one of the local news shows. One of the sportscasters has acne scars, and she tells me, "I have to cake him, I swear—a quarter of an inch." She holds up her thumb and forefinger to show me how thick his foundation has to be. In a hushed voice she reveals that the evening anchorwoman has down on her cheeks, "Like sideburns—I almost told her to shave the other day, but

I want to keep this job. It's a piece of cake," she says, reaching for another cookie. "I can do it *forever*. I can be fat, pregnant, covered with warts—who cares? I just have to make other people look good. I'm sick of jobs where you have to take care of yourself. Even a waitress has to shave her legs and suck in her belly—and waitresses are the lowest of the low."

I nod but I don't agree. I'm "taking care of myself" this week, trying to avoid being fat and covered with warts. It has to do with my new job. I work with a psychologist at Boston University who's studying appearance and self-esteem. He has a thousand slides—kids with protruding brows and no chins, ears too low or no ears at all, kids with scabby growths that cover half their faces. Then there are the "normal" ones—pictures of children with crooked teeth and big noses, wide-spaced eyes or misaligned jaws.

I show these slides to college students and they rate the children for attractiveness. Then I photograph the students to see if there is any correlation between their appearance and the way they judge others. Later, I put on a white lab coat and take wax casts of their teeth. The psychologist thinks that the mouth and chin matter most. A kid can get by with a bumpy nose but not with buckteeth.

Sometimes the college boys flirt with me. They are cocky and long-legged, unintentionally seductive as they sprawl in the chair in front of me. They call me "Doctor" when I wear the lab coat, teasing me until I slip the soft wax in their mouths and say, "Bite down." This silences them, of course, and they do not recover. When I'm done, they skulk away, shoulders curved, thumbs hooked in belt loops. This is the closest I come to romance, these meaningless flirtations I must destroy.

At home I often stare in the mirror for an hour or more, but I never look at my whole face; I study it in parts. The eyes are gray and the lashes pale, unremarkable but the right distance apart and perfectly in line. I scan lips, skin, nose, looking for flaws or traces of beauty. There are none. Feature by feature, I realize I bear no resemblance to my sister, but sometimes, by accident, when I catch my reflection in a store window, there is a gesture, an angle of the head or the hips that is unmistakably Grace. I have decided my ears are my finest attribute. The lobes are pink and fleshy but not too large. Inside, the whorls are perfect as pale shells worn to a sheen by salt water.

Claudia was supposed to cook me dinner, but she falls asleep, bloated and groggy from her overdose of sugar. Her hands rest on her belly, rising and falling with each snore. I crack open a window before I leave; she needs air.

Outside, the night is heavy with the musk of magnolia. I walk slowly toward Charles, where I can hop a train to Somerville. I stop in the Public Garden, in front of my favorite sculpture, the monument to the discovery of ether. A patient lies limp and free of pain in the doctor's arms, just as Christ lay across his mother's lap, head thrown back, arms dangling. The bearded doctor swabs the patient's chest with his cool stone rag. ". . . inhaling ether causes insensibility to pain," I read. This is Boston's *pietà*, a memorial to misery and redemption.

"I do not have a bad life." This is my exact thought as I walk down the quiet street in Somerville, where nothing ever happens. I plan to live here a long time. Here there are no doormen or buzzers, no chains or double locks. "I am safe here," I think as I climb the stairs. That's when I realize my door is cracked open, the lock popped. What do I have left to steal? A rhinestone brooch, a black-and-white television, a photograph of my mother at thirty, a smiling girl full of hope.

I push the door with my fingertips, afraid to know what's gone. I can smell the intruder in my living room as if he has just stepped in front of me. I know he is still here. I resist the lights. Darkness is my friend, my advantage: this is my house. I have a crazy thought that the thief is one of the boys from the experiment, a kid who wants to pay me back for the humiliation he suffered when I shoved the wax between his teeth.

I slink along the wall to the kitchen, where I know the ironing board is still standing, where the cool iron sits, unplugged, another friend. I am watching myself, thinking: Run, run while there is still time, run before you kill the stranger in your house, but I want to kill him, to punish him for forcing his way through my door.

I have my hands on the iron when he moves, a shadow near the refrigerator; just a boy, I think, but no less dangerous for that. I am walking toward him, the iron raised, fear binding me to finish what I've begun.

Then I hear a wild peal, a cackle, and I know my sister. She bursts from her own shadow, falling into my arms, and I cry out, "I could have killed you. I could have fucking killed you."

She hugs me in the dark, her smell strong, unwashed but familiar. I cannot hug her back, not until the anger drains, a slow trickle of sweat down my spine, not until my rigid muscles go limp and I feel only the poison that panic leaves in the body. And I wonder: Did I sense all along that the shadow in my house was Grace? Even as I grabbed the iron, did the hot flame of recognition drive me toward her?

Grace grabs my face and kisses me on the mouth. She cares nothing for the moment we've just escaped, nothing for my rage or the knowledge of what I might have done.

I say it again, a murmur this time: "I almost killed you."

"But you didn't," she says. "You didn't."

ABOUT THE AUTHOR

MELANIE RAE THON is the author of *Meteors in August*, a novel. She was born in Kalispell, Montana, and now lives in Cambridge, Massachusetts. In 1980 she won a Hopwood Award for Major Fiction at the University of Michigan. She teaches writing, literature and history at several universities in the Boston area.